CREEPIN' WITH A MARRIED MILLIONAIRE

EVONNA

D1714933

Creepin' With A Married Millionaire

Copyright © 2023 by Evonna

All rights reserved.

Published in the United States of America.

Mailing List

To stay up to date on new releases, plus get information on contests, sneak peeks, and more,

Go To The Website Below...

www.colehartsignature.com

CHAPTER ONE
WAYNE

"Oh hell no! What the fuck y'all doing up in here?" I heard my wife, Shaniece, screaming. I could tell by her tone that whoever was there was not a threat, but they definitely weren't welcomed. It was obvious that she wasn't happy to see them. I immediately assumed it was the police and started locking my stashes. I could hear them getting closer and closer, leaving me just enough time to shut down the surveillance monitors before Shaniece knocked on my door.

"We got it from here!" I heard a man say to my wife.

"I don't need y'all telling me how to run my shit! Y'all ain't even supposed to be here. I ain't finna let y'all do anything to mine!" Shaniece started going off. I immediately rushed to open the door. Knowing my wife, she would start a revolution right outside of my office.

"It's coo, baby," I assured her. I placed a kiss on her forehead before fully opening the door and inviting the men in. I knew right away who they were and I was dying to hear what they had to say this time. But I had a damn good idea.

One thing I can say about myself is that I'm always ten steps ahead. There was really nothing that happened in life that I wasn't prepared for. I knew I would have haters and I knew exactly how they were going to come. It didn't surprise me even a little bit that the chief of police and the little flunky Detective Randolph were back in my office demanding that I shut down my business.

"With all due respect, we run one of the most reputable funeral services on the West Coast." I started to speak, but Shaniece took the mic.

"Not only that, but we pay our taxes and we have done more than just give back to the community. I don't understand why y'all keep bothering us," my wife said seriously, looking both men in their eyes. In most cases, a woman would be expected to let her man speak, but not this one. They had been coming after me for the last year and it was only getting worse. My wife was sick of it and so was I.

"Don't give us that bullshit!" Connor, the chief of police, yelled. I could tell he had a personal vendetta against me, but he wasn't about to take it out on my wife.

"You can lower your motherfuckin' voice tho'." I checked him immediately. I didn't give a damn about him being chief of police because if he could put me in jail I would've already been locked up. They had a couple moles who were, of course, dead now, hearsay and suspicions. They didn't have shit on me and we all knew it.

"How about you let us men talk, huh?" he replied sarcastically, as if to say I needed Shaniece to stand up for me. I laughed barely underneath my breath. Me and Shaniece watched him become even more angry about my decision to give him a chuckle as a response. He was damn near foaming at the mouth, he was so mad. His face was red as hell like he was turning into the devil himself. He was so hot that he was actually sweating.

"I know about your little side hustle!" he hissed. I shook my head at his jealousy-filled outburst. See, Connor was the chief of police but he wasn't the chief of police. He didn't give a damn about his job, all he cared about was the power and perks that came with it. He didn't want my business shut down because he felt like it was doing more harm than help. He wanted it shut down because he knew I was slowing his money up. It's kinda hard to make drug busts when you can't find the drugs. All the dirty cops who had their hands in the drug world were coming up short due to my little side operation. So in Connor's eyes, I was really a threat. Shit, I was a threat in a lot of people's eyes, but Connor hated me. He had done everything in his power to stop me and none of it had worked.

"You think you know some shit but you're really just guessing," I told him.

"Oh yeah? You think I'd waste my time coming here off a hunch?" he asked in a threatening tone. He was clearly trying to make me sweat but I wasn't going.

"I don't know! But we both know you wouldn't waste any time arresting me." I paused to let what I was about to say hit him harder.

"IF you could!" I shot back at him with a sarcastic glare.

"Key word, IF!" Shaniece popped back in.

"You see a black man doing well and assume there is some fuckery going on. Y'all always say we're doing some illegal shit but don't ever come with the evidence. We do one hell of a job and we're not going to quit because the chief here has a hard-on for my husband," she added.

"What if we asked you to sell Wettler's?" Detective Randolph pitched in, as if he had just come up with the solution to the problem they were trying to make. He could tell my wife was getting up under Connor's skin and that tough-guy shit wasn't getting them anywhere with us.

"Did you see a for sale sign out there when you walked in?" I asked in a suggestive manner, still with a hint of sarcasm. They had to be dumber than I thought if they believed we were about to sell them our business so they could harvest all of our crops.

"Look, Mrs. Wettler, I'll pay you two million dollars for the building. It's becoming a pain to the community with all the complaints. One day shit's going to hit the fan. You might as well avoid all that and walk free while you still got the chance," he said, thinking I was supposed to hop all over that offer. I made that kind of money doing my own thing. I would be a fool to settle for an offer that low.

"Are we finished here?" I asked matter-of-factly.

"Just think it over," he added before placing his business card on my desk. He smiled politely and walked to the door. Connor moved quickly behind him with a girly ass frown on his face. I exhaled the moment they walked out. It was like a breath of fresh air, except the air wouldn't be fresh for long because I knew they would be coming back.

CHAPTER TWO

SHANIECE

"Where are you going, Dwayne?" I hissed at my husband after he came back out of his office with his keys and whatnot.

"You don't need to leave right now. We need to just lay back, because those motherfuckers are probably watching your every move," I tried to explain to him how I felt, but I could tell right away he wasn't hearing anything I had to say.

"Can you just let me handle this?" he snapped.

"I don't want you out there. Them cops don't give a fuck 'bout us. They killing us for fun and you're one of their biggest fuckin' targets."

"Man, fuck them cops, fuck all that shit. Ain't nobody controlling how I move," he yelled, instantly pissing me off. He always wanted to be hot headed when he was mad, instead of thinking logically.

"All I'm saying is, don't put yourself in the line of fire," I said in a calming tone. I knew he was going to leave anyway and the last thing I wanted to do was add to his anger.

"Go home. I'll call you in a second," he said dryly before kissing me and trying to walk out the door. I was so desperate to keep him in the house that I dropped down to my knees right there in front of him.

"Please come with me!" I said as I started unbuckling his pants. He was set in his ways but he wasn't turning down any head. He accepted it graciously and I bobbed away until he was oozing love juices down my throat.

"Shit!!" he said as he leaned back on his desk. I could tell I had him weak in the knees and I was proud about it.

"Stay?" I asked in a pouting manner. I could tell right away from the look on his face that he was still determined to go. So I gave up.

"I'll see you when you get home," I said with an attitude before letting him go.

Now, don't get me wrong, my man loves and respects my opinion. He's just very unreceptive when he's upset or in his feelings. I couldn't blame him either because the cops and other officials had been bothering us nonstop. Even the damn fire department was trying to give us violations and other bullshit. It was like the entire city was against us and I hated it.

I had to worry about my husband being hurt or thrown away in jail every day. If it wasn't by somebody on the streets, I would have to worry about the police. What made it even worse is it wasn't behind my husband's bullshit. It never was!

Dwayne was smart. He never brought problems to the business and still, we were under fire. We had been in business for fifteen years with no issues. Life was never this way for us until my husband started dealing with Choice on the business side.

Of course, my husband didn't see it that way. He felt his problems were his problems. He wasn't the type to point his finger at someone, especially someone he loved. But a blind man could see, Choice was the problem.

Choice was my youngest stepson. He wasn't shit but a little young punk who lived off my husband. He had a younger brother named Chosen who was extremely close with my niece, Vera. I always felt like they were messing around but nobody else claimed to see it.

Dwayne's ex-wife and I used to be good friends up until she ended up dying in a car accident a few years back. It was a Saturday night and we both had been drinking. Because I was driving and I survived, I always blamed myself. Everybody blamed me.

So naturally, I had a soft spot for her children. I mean, I loved them both dearly, but Chosen was my favorite. Choice was a little older and understood that I should have been dead with his mother, and he wasn't too happy about it. Choice treated me like a murderer who had killed his mother and took her place. But Chosen was different. Chosen treated me like a mother. I loved me some Chosen, and eventually I started loving me some Dwayne too.

Most people think Dwayne and I were already messing around before Sheena passed away, but I'm here to say we weren't. I had never even looked at Dwayne in that way. Sheena was my real friend. I would have never crossed her and she hadn't ever crossed me. It's just that losing her took such a big toll on all of us. Dwayne was there for me like no other. And when you mix those emotions with the support he was coming with and a little liquor, you end up married to your best friend's husband.

Over time we became more and more like a family of sorts. Dwayne helped me take over my father's business after he passed away. My family had run that funeral home for generations and it had never done as good as it was doing under me and my husband. Life was good for us. Until that damn Choice would come around.

Choice only came when he needed something. On top of that, he always came with a problem or caused one. In attempts to help keep him out of trouble and get him on his shit, my husband allowed him to come work with us. Everything was just fine until he started getting hip to the side businesses. My husband was a street nigga at heart so he always managed a way to bring in some extra dollars. He wasted no time using the crematorium to smuggle drugs for the biggest drug dealers in the country.

At first I was upset because I felt like he was disrespecting the dead by stuffing their bodies with drugs and driving them around before they were finally put to rest. But after I saw the type of money the side business brought in, I just shut up and minded my business. Choice, however, couldn't do that. He had to get his hand stuck in that honey pot, and that's when all hell started to break loose.

He had this nappy-headed thang named Trice that raised hell anytime he pissed her off. One time he cheated on her inside the funeral home and she found out and came for the whole company behind it. My family's company that Choice didn't even contribute a dollar to.

She called the police and told them that we were smuggling drugs through our clients' bodies. We had cops everywhere asking us questions, and they even came back with warrants to search later. Luckily, we had time to clean everything up before they came. Lord knows we all would've been sitting up under the jail and Choice would be out with that nappy-headed Trice running free, ruining somebody else's shit.

The thought alone did not sit right with me. Me and Dwayne had dedicated so much of our lives to getting our family out the hood. The side business was never a part of the plan. But it damn sure came in handy. I mean, it put us at least ten years ahead of the game based on predictions from what we were making before then. We were so close to our goal that I was seriously considering cutting the side business off and keeping the morgue and funeral home running. We were even making additions, which were going to include a bar and restaurants for families to host their repast, balloon releases, and other things of that nature. There was literally no stopping us. We were literally millionaires.

The side business had recently been manifesting a lot of problems and bringing us a lot of threats. The money was good, but the more money we made the more problems we had. It wasn't worth the risk, especially with hot-headed motherfuckers like Choice in the equation. I didn't want to lose my family business and I didn't want any of us to go to jail. It was time to hang up the gloves and move on with our lives.

The only problem with that was going to be trying to convince my husband that we needed to move on. After making so much money and getting away with so much, Dwayne was starting to feel invincible. It was starting to feel like this would be our life forever. I hadn't even heard him mention us getting away from the hood lately and that's usually all he talked about. Every other day it was 'we're going to move here' or 'we're going to move there.' That was before the madness though. Now all he talked about was making more money, buying more businesses, and getting more established in the hood instead of leaving.

Once those dollars started coming in, my husband started drifting further and further from the plan. I could tell it was all about the business now. Don't get me wrong, I know my husband loves me and our family. I just think he might love getting money more. Just a little.

Either way, I knew it wasn't going to be easy trying to get him to cut ties with the game. And that was the scary part because we were already considered filthy rich. The world says money is the root of all evil but in another dimension, greed is the root of all evil.

CHAPTER THREE
CHOICE

I set outside of the address this little baddie named Shawnie had given me. She was dropped dead gorgeous and any man would come right out they pocket to have her. I know I would. She was dark with almond eyes and the body of a goddess. But that wasn't what had me pulling up on her. I had just met her at Wettler's. She worked for the transportation service. She was literally the missing piece of my puzzle. If I could lock her in, my little side business was going to soar to a new level. And that's exactly what I was about to do.

"You can come up. I'm about to come open the door." She said once I called her to announce my arrival.

She came to the door looking like a meal. I swear I could've ate her up right then and there. I could tell from the way she was looking at me that she would let me have my way with her. But as a man I was going to try and keep the shit strictly business between us.

"We can go to my study." She informed me as she took off walking through her house. Her place was nice, real laid back and I could tell she lived alone. I liked that because it suggested that she knew how to be private when necessary.

"You want to travel the world in style, huh?" i asked, looking at a golden globe she had sitting on her desk. I lifted my finger up as if I was about to touch it and a small part of her went crazy.

"Please! Have a seat." She blurted out the first thing that came to her mind. She actually sounded polite but I could tell from her body language that she was offended.

"Im sorry. My son gave me that. He went missing a few weeks ago. So I'm very picky about this globe." She explained.

"My apologies baby. I'm sorry to hear about your son. I didn't know." I said immediately regretting my decision to acknowledge the globe. She looked at me like she was overly pleased with my response. I watched her nipples harden as she started biting her bottom lip. It's like she was turned on by my presence alone. I kept thinking about what was at stake with her. I wasn't trying to fuck her hood then that get in the way of my goal.

"I changed my mind." I said matter of factly.

"What do you mean?" She asked offensively, knowing she hadn't did anything wrong to me.

"I mean, I changed my mind. I was trying to put you on this little hustle I got. But I think ima have to find somebody else."

"When did you decide that and why? We haven't even discussed the details."

"People are going to see what I can do to you and they're going to be alarmed. I don't want to do anything to jeopardize your job."

"What do you mean what you can do to me?" She asked confused.

"I just changed your whole mood." I told her.

"You just was ready to snap on me and calmed down

soon as I spoke. Our energy so raw together that I just watched it melt your frustration. I actually just had you speechless for a second and I wasn't even trying to." I stated my observations.

"Speechless?" Shawnie laughed nervously. She didn't have to admit that she felt differently in my presence because I could see it.

"I don't know what your point is but you better hurry up and make it because I'm not going to continue to waste my time."

"Waste your time?" I repeated her last statement. I couldn't believe the words she had said to me. I reached in to his pocket and pulled out a small wad of money.

"I've been here for an hour." I said handing her the money. She took it and looked up at me not exactly sure of why I was giving her the money.

"I ain't trying to waste your time. You cant tell me that you ain't feel what I just felt." I continued to try to wrap her around my finger.

"Feel what? What are you talking about?" She was playing clueless.

"I don't know Shawnie. I never felt it. But I like it and I want some more."

"So, is this like love at first sight or something?" She asked rolling her eyes.

I could tell she was thinking I was just some street nigga who wanted her fine ass under my belt.

"It could be love at first sight." I said while matter-of-factly, licking my lips.

"I never been in love before. It could be a very strong case of lust. Whatever it is, I want some more." I confessed while stepping closer to her.

She acted like she wanted to tell me not to get so close but her lips didn't move. And pretty soon i had my hands cupping her face.

"Shawnie." I whispered her name as I looked in to her eyes. She nearly fainted trying to keep her composure under my spell. I pulled her face in to my chest and cradled her there.

"I meet a lot of women. But I've never seen in them what I seen in you today. I'm intrigued. I want to know more about you." I whispered directly in to her ear while caressing her arms and shoulders.

"I asked to meet with you so we could do business. I wanted to just kind of get an idea of who you are and what that vibe was about. But this is way better."

"What do you mean this is better?" Shawnie asked.

"Being able to touch you, smell you, just vibing with you dolo is good enough for me. You bad for real. I want you to call me." I confessed before placing a kiss on her forehead. She stared up at me unsure.

"I don't date my business partners." She replied with what she thought was the right answer.

"I'll leave my card here with you. When you get ready, call me. I'll be waiting."

"What makes you so certain that I'm going to call you?" She decided to pick my brain a little.

Her mind was blown when I made the decision to lift her face up and kiss her on her neck. She started to fight it at first but for reasons unknown to myself, she just gave in to me. I lifted her up on to her desk and slid her dress up.

"I know what I'm talking about." I whispered as he slowly slid my hand up her legs and between her thighs.

"You feel that?" I whispered as i massaged her clit through her panties.

"Yes! Yes I feel it." She moaned as i pleased her with just my fingers. Her moan was sexy as fuck. It damn near sent me into overdrive.

I slid his fingers into her love box and began twirling them around. I knew exactly which spots of hers to hit. She moaned a little louder and i started gently choking her and biting on her shoulders. Her reaction let me know she liked that rough shit. That turnt me on even more.

"Somebody's backed up." I whispered as she melted in my arms.

"Let me get it." I begged. She had me so wrapped up that I was kissing her on the lips. And I never did that with anyone but my wife. Shawnie shook her head in disagreement but her lips screamed out the word yes. Her body was begging for me and no matter how much she told herself it was wrong I know it felt right. It felt damn good. So good that she wasn't about to stop it. She was craving it.

"You see what I was talking about?" I asked, abruptly ending the little finger tease show i had just put on for her.

"If I can get all of that up out of you, I definitely can get a phone call." I said referring to the creamy juices that Shawnie had dripped all on my finger. I stuck my fingers inside her mouth and watch lustfully as she cleaned her own juices off my finger.

"You're going to be mines. Watch!" I said before confidently exiting her home.

CHAPTER FOUR
TRICE

I heard the sound of my husband's system banging from all the way down the street. Every molecule in my body started to jump up and down with excitement. I absolutely loved everything about Choice. He and I had been together for about seven years and we'd been married for about three. We both had done everything you could think of together, both good and bad. But no matter what, we never let go of each other! Most people will call it toxic, but if you could feel the way he made me feel, you would know that it was love. Real love.

I rushed to the bathroom to check myself in the mirror to make sure I was looking nothing less than flawless. My man kept my hair and nails done so there was never much for me to do. All I had to do was the little things. I applied some lipgloss to my luscious lips and reapplied some mousse to my bouncy curls. I was already in my panties and bra, so I just threw on a cute little silk robe. That way he still had the panty and bra set to look forward to. After one more glance in the mirror, I was good. I sprayed on some perfume and went to meet my man at the door.

Choice walked in looking like a million bucks. He was a Cali boy at heart. He liked Dickies suits and Chuck Taylor's, but nobody could put that shit on like him though. I swear, my man did it like nobody else. I licked my lips as he walked up, staring at his juicy lips. His skin seemed to shimmer under the sun, as if the sun gods themselves had kissed him. The scent of his cologne graced me as I waited lustfully for him to be in my arms' reach. His jewelry shined like the sun. And his swag was as cold as winter. He was just one sexy ass motherfucker.

"Hey, baby," I said to him as I tooted my butt out and puckered up my lips. I was expecting him to be as happy to see me as I was to see him. But I quickly figured out that I was wrong.

"Bitch, get the fuck off me!" Choice barked at me as he pushed me away from him. I looked at him, confused about his reaction to me, until I saw a couple of his homeboys about to come in behind him.

"I got company and you walking around this bitch like they are here for you," he added, almost sounding as if he was heartbroken. I immediately shook my head and started explaining myself.

"Baby, I'm so sorry! I didn't know that you were having company. I'll go upstairs and change right now!" I replied obediently.

"Just go upstairs and stay there. If you bring your ass down the stairs while they are here again, we're going to have a problem!" Choice said seriously. I looked at his eyes and saw that they were dilated beyond normal. That meant he was high. Choice had a dark desire for cocaine. It turned him into a completely different person. And I could not stand that motherfucker.

Without another word, I hurried back upstairs into the bedroom, just like my husband told me to do. Of course, the fact that he told me not to come back downstairs raised my antennae. I knew that had to mean that he had something up his sleeve. And knowing Choice, it was either some grimy job or something to do with some bitches. Either way, I wanted to know about it.

Eager to see what I was missing, I snatched my phone and opened up our surveillance app. It gave me access to every room in our house. I was actually able to see and hear everything Choice and his boys were doing.

"I don't think you niggas understand how serious of a play this is! We got to take this shit seriously," Choice told his homeboys, Marty and Quan. He was sweating as if he was playing a basketball game with three seconds left on the clock. But I knew that it was just from him being high off cocaine.

"When I tell you it's enough for us all to eat, I'm telling you that we are all going to be straight. Our kids are even going to be straight. And the best part about it is, we're not even taking any risk," Choice added as he went back to his drugs. I shook my head in disgust. I loved him but I hated who he became when he was high. He wasn't the same person. My husband being hooked on cocaine was the one thing keeping us from getting our happily ever after.

"How are you gonna say we ain't taking a risk and we're literally burning bodies?" Marty asked, clearly confused about Choice's logic.

"It's hella risk involved. You talking 'bout life!" he added.

"Shit, fuck the police. We taking a risk with your dad for real," Quan added with a little tone of bitch in his voice.

"Right!" Marty jumped back in.

"That nigga is one of the most respected niggas in the south. He's basically untouchable. We are definitely taking a risk," he said, shaking his head.

"Man, shut yo' bitch ass up!" Choice snapped. "They don't even know who y'all are. Shit, they're not going to know that you're there. Trust me, we're not taking any risk," Choice assured his paranoid friends.

"How can you be so sure of that?" Quan decided to put another two cents in. He knew that Wayne was a big dog in the field and he really wasn't trying to take the chances of getting on his bad side. Especially not for somebody like Choice.

"One of my little shorties I be fucking with works with transport. She gone make it to where y'all can drive the trucks. All y'all gotta do is make a stop, drop some of that shit off, and get the shipment there on time," Choice assured them.

I watched as he broke down his whole plan. I was getting madder and madder by the second, because why the hell did he have to fuck a bitch to get a job done? Why was he even desperate for more when his father gave us everything we could ever ask for? That's the drug thing I was talking 'bout. He just turned into a dumb ass off that shit.

"Transport is its own company. They have no knowledge of the side business. My shorty gone give us one of the trucks whenever we need it. There ain't gone be no risk for y'all because they don't even know who you are. We got the best way to pick up bodies and move as much dope as the streets need!" Choice added positively.

I sat back and shook my head at my devious ass husband. It was so like him to try to take his father down a couple notches. Choice always wanted more. He was a king and could never settle in any situation. And I was fine with that, but what was getting me was the fact that he was fucking with some bitch to make it happen.

Still, she wasn't a threat. I already knew enough about her to have her wiped out of the game and I didn't even know who she was yet. The moment that bitch thought she was gone become a problem for me with my man, I was going to report her ass back to Wayne and Shaniece. She wouldn't last a second as Choice's 'shorty,' as he called her. And if she did, I would still be waiting on his ass too. That's just how the fuck I got down. I always got the last laugh. Everybody knew that.

"Alright, we gotta wrap this up because that nigga Chosen is about to come inside. But y'all do see it's a bulletproof plan, right?" Choice asked his boys.

Both men nodded in agreement like the peons they were. I smiled to myself, knowing that Chosen would flip the fuck out if he knew what Choice and his dirty ass friends were planning. Chosen was mad crazy over Shaniece's niece, Vera. She was more like Shaniece's daughter as Shaniece had taken her in as a child. You could never catch her without Chosen right behind her. He loved her and he loved Shaniece. But he really loved his father. There was no way Chosen would ever let Choice do some high ass bullshit like he was planning and everybody knew it.

"No matter what y'all niggas do, don't say anything about this shit to nobody. And definitely don't speak on it after Chosen comes," Choice warned them one more time before moving on to his next topic.

CHAPTER FIVE
CHOICE

I hit a few more lines of cocaine as I sat in my car trying to get my thoughts together. I had so much planned out but so much more I needed to do. I knew that I was plugged in good for now, but I was thinking about longevity. I needed to make sure that I was secure for the long run, and my dad was the solution to my problems.

My dad had let me see a little too much. He was literally making millions of dollars while I was struggling not to go under the twenty-band mark. There was no way possible I wasn't about to get some of that money. Shit, if anything, he owed me that money.

See, my dad had always been loyal to me, and from the outside looking in you would think he was the perfect father. And he was, but he wasn't the perfect man. He was loyal to me but not my mother. His wife, the woman he vowed to love forever. No way my momma died because Shaniece wanna drink and drive and my dad was okay with it.

My mother was a homebody, she barely went out. She stayed home with us every day damn near. Shaniece was the party animal and she gets to live while my mom dies? Then she goes on to stop drinking and partying and marries my father? That bitch thinks she can become my mother and she can't. And I can't respect my dad for even allowing the bitch to try that shit. So no matter how much I love my father and how much he did for me and Chosen, a small part of me was always feeling like "fuck Wayne!"

All bullshit aside, though, I knew how to play my role. I knew that the guilt of my mom's death and the weight of his marriage with Shaniece would put me closer to his grace than anyone else could ever get. And I was OK with that. I wasn't going to try to take him down. I was just going to take enough to set me and my family straight. And with the type of money that he and Shaniece were making, he probably wouldn't even notice anything missing. I wasn't going to try to take an entire shipment but I was definitely going to be piecing off whatever I could get my hands on.

Of course, I had other hustles too. Shawnie had recently introduced me to this jeweler who specialized in jewelry heists. He was an older guy from Moscow. His name was Raj. I met him doing a job with Marty, he paid well, and always came through with the best jobs. This last job he put us on, we hit a jewelry store. We banked millions of dollars' worth of jewelry. Raj cut us both a half a mil and gave us each a couple pounds of jewelry. Anything we wanted, just not his diamonds. But I was cool with that. I respected how he did business and definitely wanted to keep doing business with him.

The moment I was able to talk to him without Marty being around, I put him up on the game. I let him know that we could smuggle anything for him through the funeral home for a reasonable fee. And just as I expected, he needed transportation for a ton of things. Needless to say, I quickly learned that I could pinch from Raj and my dad all at the same damn time. And that was exactly what I was about to do.

"What's up with my OG?" I said once I stepped inside of my dad's office. His office would remind you of an architect's, of sorts. The entire place screamed money. In fact, just being in his office always motivated me. It was just proof that I could be doing better. I was going to get there though.

"Hey Choice! What's up with my young bull" He said back to me. I could tell from his tone that he was genuinely happy to see me. He always seemed genuinely happy to see me. But that didn't change the past. I wasn't about to let that soften me up. I was still going to stick to my plan.

"I have a proposal for you," I said enthusiastically. I knew that he would hop all over the proposal because he loved the money too much. The fact that he trusted me was enough to get Raj in the door. And once I had his permission to do business with Raj, I was better enabled to continue to pull off my other side hustles. Once I got him in the door, everything was up for grabs.

"I've been doing this work for this Russian cat," I began to explain my proposal for him. I knew it was important that I chose my words wisely. I didn't want to say anything that would alarm him. I knew he loved money more than anything in the world, but pleasing his wife was definitely a priority for him as well. He couldn't afford to lose her because she was a big part of his lifeline financially. We all knew the company was really hers and he was just in the whip with her. So anything that sounded too hot, he would pass up on.

"His name is Raj. He needs help transporting diamonds and jewelry and he's willing to pay $500 per pound. With a minimum of ten grand every trip," I explained with a greedy smile on my face. I was also sure to add a little greed in the tone of my voice. I knew if my dad could see how big of a deal I thought things were, that he would most likely consider the plan.

"You know, not too many folks can bring me business nowadays," my dad said seriously as he poured us both a shot of cognac from his office bar.

"But you're not too many folks!" he said with a smile on his face that let me know he was about to fall right into my plan.

"We will give him two trips in one week. If everything goes right and there's no funny business, we can think about doing something long term with him," my dad added enthusiastically.

"Trust me, there's no funny business. You have my word on it," I assured him as I tossed back the glass of cognac he had given me.

"Good! Because if anything does go wrong, it's falling solely on you!" he said seriously. I knew that was a sugar-coated threat. My dad loved me too much to threaten me directly. Still, it was what it was. I knew better than anybody not to take any threat from him lightly.

CHAPTER SIX

WAYNE

The moment Choice stepped out of my office, I started doing my homework on this Raj guy. It wasn't that I didn't trust Choice—he was my son and I loved him —that's just how I operated. I didn't trust anyone. Especially with the damn police trying to hit me from every which angle they possibly could. I had way too much to lose to be taking risks. Anything I was involved in, I needed to be sure that I didn't have to worry about any bullshit.

I pulled out my phone and dialed my wife's number. She was the main person I trusted with my life. She was so smart that she could literally find out anything about a person. All I had to do was give her something to go off. That's another thing I loved about her. Shaniece was really every woman. There wasn't anything that I could ask for that she wouldn't give me. She was just that type of woman.

"What do you want, boy?" she answered her phone with an attitude that instantly put a smile on my face. She was so sassy and fierce and I loved that shit. I simply couldn't get enough of it. Her attitude was so sexy. She was mad at me because she felt like the side business was getting a little too much out of hand. I showed her over and over that I had shit under control. But she still felt some type of way. And I understood, honestly, because that funeral home was her family's legacy. Hell, that was one of the main reasons I even married her before falling in love with her. The place was a gold mine so I understood her fear of losing it.

"Come on baby, don't be that way," I said to her with a smile on my face. She paused for a moment, and I could literally feel her smiling over the phone. That's how strong our love and energy was for each other. We were soulmates. We could literally read each other without being in the same room.

"What do you want, boy?" she repeated herself. This time she had a little bit more sass to it. I could tell she just wanted an apology, and I wasn't about to make her wait for one. Shaniece and Vera being happy was one of my main priorities. And whenever one of them wasn't happy, my life was literally hell.

"Look baby, I know you're upset and you have every right to be. I don't want you to feel like I'm not hearing you out. I just want you to give me space to do what I need to do for us," I said in a genuinely apologetic tone. She paused again. I could tell that things were really bothering her because of how fast the topic could change her moods. I didn't want her feeling like I wasn't paying attention to what she was saying. I just didn't need her trying to run everything. There was certain shit she just wasn't supposed to be a part of and she didn't understand that.

"Baby, you don't understand! I have a bad feeling about Choice. I really just don't think you should be doing business with him. He's bringing too much heat our way." She sighed.

"Baby, I hear you. And I don't need you to worry about

that. Choice is my son. Let me handle this, I promise you every-thing is going to be straight," I promised her. I knew that was exactly what she wanted to hear. Luckily for me, it was also the truth.

"You said we were just gonna make enough money to leave. Now it seems like you're not even focused on us leaving anymore. I feel like I'm losing you to my own fuckin' business," she said seriously. That actually hurt my soul a little bit hearing her say that because I knew she meant it. There was nothing or no one that she would ever lose me to. And the fact that she felt that way let me know that I needed to step my game up.

"Don't say no shit like that, Shaniece! We're still going to do everything we were supposed to do. Just relax," I said calmly to her. I didn't want her getting upset all over again. I made a mental note to do something very nice for her later. Then I moved right on to the next topic. "I need you to look into some things for me," I told her after hearing her breaths settle.

"What is it, baby?" she replied softly.

"Russian dude. His name is Raj. He works with jewelry. He has a few jewelry stores. I want to know what stores he owns, where he lives, and even if he has a record. Give me everything you can get on him, OK?"

"Who the hell is Raj? This better not have anything to do with that goddamned Choice either," she replied in a way that let me know her attitude was slowly creeping back in.

"Baby, I just told you I got this. Look into that for me and get dressed. I'm taking my girls out for dinner tonight." I figured the dinner invitation would settle her thoughts a little.

"I'm going to do this for you, baby. And if you're not ready in ninety days, I'm going to leave without you. I'm tired of waiting."

"Do what I told you to do, Shaniece. I'll be there around six to pick you up," I said before hanging up the phone. I didn't want to upset her but I damn sure didn't want her to upset me. And Shaniece threatening to leave me was the number one way to do that.

CHAPTER SEVEN

VERA

"I know this shit got something to do with Choice's ole grimy ass!" I heard my aunt Shaniece hiss after I walked into her front door. I stood still for a second, waiting for her to speak again so I could know which direction to look for her in. It took her about thirty seconds before she was screaming again.

"That scandalous ass little motherfucker. I don't know why my husband even deals with his little pussy ass," my aunt yelled as she hurried to stack up some newspapers that were scattered across her desk.

"Auntie, what are you in here yelling about?" I asked seriously. My auntie jumped a little bit, letting me know that I had startled her. She was so wrapped up in her thoughts that she wasn't even paying attention to her surroundings.

"Shit! You scared the hell out of me," she replied with a smile on her face. I knew her well enough to know that that smile was a symbol of her being embarrassed of not watching her surroundings.

"Are you here alone?" she asked, looking past me in search of Chosen.

I shook my head and smiled at my crazy ass auntie. She was as crazy as it could get, but I wouldn't change her for the world. She had taken me in after my mother overdosed when I was only eight. She was like a mother to me. I loved her, even though I felt like she was usually the one tripping about shit.

"Chosen isn't with me, Auntie. He's going to meet us for dinner," I explained.

"Good!" she cheered lightly. I knew she wasn't cheering about Chosen not being present. It was more so cheering for the fact that we were alone.

"I want to show you something," she added before scattering all the paper she had just stacked back up out on the desk again.

"Now, you know none of these problems came up for the side business until your father brought Choice on board, right?" my aunt asked as if she was some type of detective. She did have a point though. The business had never seen as much trouble as it had seen since Choice became a part of the team.

"Now Choice is bringing your father jobs," my aunt told me. She was noticeably frustrated and physically quoting the word 'jobs' with her hands.

"What's the jobs?" I asked, intrigued. I knew my aunt bugged out a lot, but I always cared to hear what she had to say. My aunt was an overthinker who came off kind of cuckoo to people. But I knew her. Even though she tweaked out often, I knew she wasn't crazy.

"So, this nigga asked me to look up this guy, right?" She slid a picture of a Russian elder to me before finishing her statement.

"So I looked it up and found out he is one of the biggest

jewelry smugglers in the country. Like, even the feds want his ass."

"So, why isn't he already in jail?" I asked, confused as to how this guy could be doing so much and still walking free.

"The thing is, he is so well put up that nobody can get to him."

"OK. . . Sounds like he's about his business then?" I responded, still lost as to what my aunt was tripping about.

"Yeah, but everybody he does business with ends up dead. He's not the kind of guy that's going to leave loose ends."

"So what exactly are you trying to say, Aunt Shaniece?"

"I'm telling you, I have a bad feeling about this. That damn Choice is going to bring problems that are too big for us to solve," she said with her voice cracking. It made me stop and think about what she was actually saying. In my mind, my uncle Wayne had always been the biggest and the baddest. But the way my aunt was talking was making me wonder if there was someone bigger and badder than him.

"I need you to help me get your uncle to see this. Because for whatever reason, I can't seem to get through to him when it comes to his grimy ass son," my aunt said irritably.

I stood in silence for a minute, trying to think of the words to say. I felt where she's coming from, but there was literally no way for me to convince my uncle to cut his son off. My uncle Wayne was a loyal man. He lived by the code. There was no one who could turn him against anybody except for that person themselves.

"You know how that is. You can say what you want, but he still going to go off his own feelings, Auntie. You know that!" I said the best thing I could think of. I didn't want to make her think I was fighting against her or not hearing what she had to say. And I definitely didn't want to make her think that I was taking up for Choice either.

"No, fuck that!" my auntie snapped before placing her stilettos on. "He's gonna have to learn how to go off my feelings too. We're married. This is what he signed up for!" she added before heading out the door. I hurried behind her so that we would not be late to dinner with Uncle Wayne.

"Oh god!" I said at the thought of how our dinner was about to go. I shook my head one last time as I followed behind my aunt to what I was certain was going to end up being a dinner from hell.

CHAPTER EIGHT
CHOSEN

After checking my fly out in the mirror one last time, I confirmed with myself that I was ready to go. It was always like that for me when I was about to go see Vera. I always wanted to look my best. I didn't want her to think that there was another nigga on this planet that was flier than me.

Because it was a formal dinner, I had thrown on something simple. A Dickies fit with some chocolate Timberland boots. The suit was tan so the whole hook up gave off that chocolatey peanut butter Reese's cup vibe. And anyone who knew Vera could tell you that she was absolutely crazy for Reese's cups.

I wore chocolate diamonds with my chocolate Rolex and a chocolate fitted hat to match my timbs. My waves were bussin and I knew that Vera was going to melt right out of her panties when she saw me. She was always calling me Usher, and at first I used to hate that shit. I used to feel like she was comparing me to another man, and a soft man at that. But once I realized how much she liked him and how much other women liked him, I started taking it as a compliment.

I never have been the type of man to give a fuck about my appearance for the next motherfucker, but when it came to Vera, I had to! I went out my way to melt her ass every time.

Vera and I have been friends since childhood. When her mother passed away Shaniece took her in, and with Shaniece being my mom's best friend, Vera was always around us. We have been through everything together. So much so, that by the time I hit eighteen, Vera was my girl. At least in my mind she was. She had that little fear of my father finding out, so we never fully came out with it. But motherfuckers knew she was mine. For real, I even think my dad knew, he just never spoke on it.

Either way, nothing or no one would ever be able to stop me from loving Vera. She was always going to be my baby. There was nothing that could change that. And if a mother-fucker couldn't respect that, then fuck them. And that went for everybody, including my dad.

"What's up love, where are you at?" I asked once Vera answered her phone. The sound of her voice always made me smile no matter what was going on. She's the only woman I've ever dealt with that had never lost that little effect on me.

"Hey baby, we are on the way to Geo's," Vera told me. She had already explained to me that she was going out to dinner with Shaniece and my dad. It was something we did every Sunday. Vera made sure she always reminded me, because sometimes I'd miss it. I didn't want to be suffocating or come off as overbearing to Vera but truth is, I couldn't stand being away from her.

"I think I'ma sit this one out, love," I said, joking with Vera. Her attitude shifted immediately from happy go lucky to mad as hell.

"What do you mean you're going to sit this one out?" she barked. Vera was the softest, sweetest woman you would ever meet but when she got mad, she could transform into a demon. But a sexy ass demon. It made my dick hard every time I even got a glimpse of the shit.

"I'm just playing, love," I assured her as I pulled up to Kay Jewelers. I knew my dad always bought her something every Sunday and I couldn't show up empty-handed. We had Vera used to living a certain lifestyle and I was going to show him and her that I could maintain that lifestyle for her. "I will be there in a second!" I promised her before hanging up the phone.

I quickly made my way into the jewelers so that I could grab her a nice piece really quick. The staff at the jewelry shop already knew me on a first-name basis because I spent so much money with the company. They also knew Vera really well and were more than happy to help me find her the perfect gift.

"What is the occasion?" one of the salesmen said after watching me look around for a few minutes.

"I just want to do something special for her," I said honestly. There wasn't any occasion. Vera deserved special gifts every day not occasionally. But one would have to love her to know that.

"How about we get a matching necklace for the tennis bracelet that you got her?" the man suggested, letting me know that he remembered my last purchase. I took a couple minutes to think about what he said. I really had no clue what to get her so I wasn't about to go against his word.

"Yes, let's do it," I said eagerly. I was for certain that Vera would absolutely love a necklace. Especially one that matched the tennis bracelet. She was absolutely crazy about that bracelet. After hearing that suggestion, I was certain there was nothing better that I could get for her.

After getting the necklace sized and wrapped up, I hurried

to Geo's steakhouse where Vera, my father, and Shaniece were already waiting for me. It was crazy because I had known Shaniece since I was a young pup. Yet, I still got nervous around her when it came to how to treat her.

I made it to the steakhouse in about six minutes. I made sure to spray some cologne on me before I entered the building. I knew Vera loved that shit. I wanted to be sure that I wasn't lacking in any department. I had to be on point with all of my shit for her.

Once I stepped into the restaurant, I spotted her, my dad, and Shaniece sitting at a table. The looks on their faces were perplexed, and I could tell right away that this was not a regular family dinner. Luckily, they had not seen me yet. That gave me an opportunity to watch them a little longer and see if I could get some clues as to what the hell was going on. Something definitely was not right.

"Hey, Chosen baby!" Vera cooed loudly, unintentionally fuckin' up my attempts to be nosy. I watched as my dad and Shaniece's body language changed at the sound of Vera mentioning my name.

Choice must've done something, I thought to myself as Vera ran and jumped into my arms. Her greeting was always the same to me no matter who was around. What was different this time wasn't her greeting though, it was my dad and Shaniece's. There was most definitely something going on and I was almost certain it had something to do with my brother Choice. His ass was always up to something.

CHAPTER NINE
TRICE

The sound of my phone ringing non stop woke me up from the slumber I had literally fell into. I was so hungover from drinking the night before that my head was beating like my man's system in his car. I looked over at my ringing phone and noticed it was a private number. I debated answering it for a second too long because before I could hit the answer button the phone stopped ringing.

"Who the fuck is calling me private?" I said to myself as I raised up to get completely out of bed. Before my feet could even touch the floor, my phone was ringing again.

"What?" I answered the phone annoyed with the fact that somebody thought it was okay to just blow my phone up like that.

"Bitch, lower your motherfucking tone." An unfamiliar male voice responded.

"Who the fuck is this?" I asked confused as fuck.

"Where your husband?" The man asked.

"Look, ion got time for no motherfucking games!" I snapped. I was use to people calling playing on my phone about Choice. Sometimes it would be his side bitches and sometimes it would be niggas he done pissed off that's to scared to do something to him.

"Nobody playing games bitch. If you was smart, you would take your kids and go. Dude gone end up getting y'all killed." He said in a tone that made me a little nervous.

"How ass nigga you think I give a fuck about what you saying?" I laughed.

"Bitch you wanna play? I got motherfuckers sitting outside your shit right now!" He barked. I paused for a second wondering if there was any truth in his threat. I looked out my windows and didn't see anyone. I was certain he was bluffing.

"Sounds like someone's getting a little heated." I teased him.

"You listen to me you little black bitch!" He roared. "I'll show you heated. I will burn your ass alive."

"Wow I'm trembling in my fucking panties." I laughed."

"You know what bitch, I tried to spare you. If this is how you want things to be then so be it. The wait is over." He said before abruptly ending their phone call.

I let out a sigh of relief, happy that call was over. I felt good about standing my ground with him but not so good about what the consequences might be. I had no clue who he was and if he was actually going to go through on his threats. It made me feel worried and very uneasy. I went and grabbed my gun just to feel a little safer and then I picked up her phone to call Choice. Of course he didn't answer. I knew deep down in my heart he was with another woman. He always was with someone else and never around when I needed him. I decided to call him back just to see if I would get through the second time.

Before the phone could even ring a second time, i was startled by a crashing sound somewhere in my home. Immediately, my alarm system started to fill the house with a screeching ring. "FRONT DOOR!" The alarm system continued to fill the house. "Living room motion sensor activated. Intruder! INTRUDER!"

Someone was in my house. I hurried to get behind my bedroom door so i would be able to see the intruder before they could see me. I looked down at my phone and could see that Choice hadn't answered. Not knowing who else to call, I decided to call Wayne.

"Someone just broke in my house! Call Choice and call the police." I whispered into the phone.

"Get somewhere safe and lay low. I'm about five minutes away from there." Wayne whispered as if he was in the house too. He had heard the alarm the second he answered my call. I could hear concern in his tone and the desire to protect me.

"Just stay safe until I get there." Wayne added.

I did as I was told and waited patiently on Wayne. I could hear somebody running out of my house. I wasn't sure if the alarm had ran them off or what but they were getting up out of there. I sat in silence for the next few minutes, terrified to even move until I heard Wayne's voice.

"Oh my god! Thank you!" I cried as I jumped out of hiding and ran into his arms. He held me so tightly that I involuntarily started to cry harder.

"Where are the girls?" He asked about his grandkids.

"They're not here!"

"Did they hurt you?" He asked, looking at my face and body.

"No, someone called me talking about the Yw eye going to kill us over Choice. I thought it was a prank call but he warned me he was coming in."

"What you mean he warned you?"

"He told me he had people outside. Then he said the wait is over and that's when they kicked down my door."

"Did you see anybody?"

"No."

"This sounds like a scare. They want Choice to know they know where his home is." Wayne said seriously as he started to scope out the house.

CHAPTER TEN
CHOICE

I tried to control myself as I watched Shawnie walk from her job to my car. Shawnie was bad as fuck. Real dark skin, thick as hell, just all the way around gorgeous. Just watching her sway my way was making my dick hard. Her hips were bulging out her jeans and her moose knuckle was challenging me. I wanted to get out of my car and take her ass down right in the parking lot.

"Hey Daddy!" she cooed once she hopped in my whip. She leaned over and placed a kiss on my cheek, gently caressing my dick at the same time. "He missed me?" she asked in a joking manner after feeling my shit on hard. She bent over and kissed my dick. I had on jeans but the shit still felt good. I was turned on like a motherfucker.

"We both missed you," I said with a smile.

"This is for you," she said, handing me a brown paper bag.

"What's this?" I asked, wondering what she had up her sleeve. I wasn't expecting anything from her so I was completely caught off guard.

"It's called a home-cooked meal. It's way better than all

that fast food shit you be eating with them knockoff hoes," she said sarcastically.

"Word?" I smiled at her sassiness. The fact that she thought to cook a nigga a meal was enough to make me pay her bills for the whole year.

"Let me see what you're working with!" I teased as I pulled the plate out. There was fried catfish and chicken, greens with turkey tails, macaroni and cheese, black eyed peas, and hot water cornbread.

"I know this ain't no hot water cornbread," I said, truly surprised. I hadn't had hot water cornbread since my grand-mother passed. I definitely didn't expect her to come through with some.

"Southern style," Shawnie said proudly.

I wasted no time digging into that plate. Trice's ass barely ever cooked anymore so I was definitely overdue for a home-cooked meal.

"Damn, you acting like you ain't ate in years!" Shawnie laughed. I smiled at her as I continued to demolish the food she had made for me. She didn't even know that that plate was enough to get me hooked.

"I haven't!" I replied jokingly as I licked the juices from her food off my fingers.

"And I haven't had any pussy either," I said seriously. But she and I both knew I was joking. I got pussy whenever I wanted. Everybody knew that.

"Did you come here for pussy or business?" Shawnie asked me seriously.

It fucked me up a little because as serious as she was she still licked her lips at me and leaned forward toward me in a promising way. I hadn't fucked her yet but her body language let me know that I could, and that let me know that I would.

"I came here for you. But we're definitely gonna make sure we get this business shit together!"

"Your mother never told you not to mix business with pleasure?" she asked in a sarcastic yet still flirtatious tone. The fact she even mentioned my mom made a tiny piece of me mad as hell.

"My mother is dead," I said seriously, in a way that warned her not to ever try some "your momma" shit with me again. For a moment, the car grew silent and all you could hear was the sound of me smacking on her food.

"I didn't mean anything by that. I didn't know," Shawnie said sincerely. I could tell she meant every word she said, but I wasn't about to let her know that. I was about to make her feel bad now so she could break her neck to be nice to me later.

"It's all good," I said dryly as I finished up the last of my plate. "Besides, you're right! I shouldn't be trying to mix business with pleasure no way," I told her before quickly switching the subject back to strictly business. My phone started ringing, rudely interrupting our conversation.

"I gotta take this!" I told Shawnie after seeing it was my dad calling. She nodded silently and stepped out of the car.

"Wassup old g?" I answered my phone.

"Wassup is motherfuckers just broke in your house trying to kill your family." He snapped.

"What the fuck you talking about?" I asked confused as to what the hell he was talking about. I lived way in the cut. My family was so well put up that I was confident none of my opponents would ever be able to hunt us down.

"Exactly what the fuck I said. Now I don't know what your ass is out here doing but you better handle this shit. Because if I got to handle it me and you gone have a problem." He said before hanging up the phone.

CHAPTER ELEVEN
SHANIECE

After realizing that my husband was not taking my warnings about his sneaky ass son seriously, I started to take matters into my own hands. It wasn't that I didn't trust my husband, it was just that I was concerned. Wayne could lead an army to victory alone. Everyone knew that. But Wayne didn't have that woman's instinct that I had. I knew he was going to try to handle things his way and I was going to allow him to. Just not until I took a few more precautions.

I had overheard my husband and Choice saying that they were going to go meet with Raj. They wouldn't be back for at least a couple hours. That gave me more than enough time to put a few things together. I knew that my husband didn't consider his son a threat, but I did. I could feel his disloyalty in my bones. There were little voices in my head literally screaming for me to get my family away from him. And I absolutely had to find a way to get my husband to hear those same voices.

I had additional security cameras hidden throughout the

entire funeral home. I even went so far as hiding them in the actual morgue. I knew that damn Choice would eventually do something against my husband's wishes and whenever he did, I was going to have it on camera. In addition to that, I went through all the orders of the past week. I noticed right away that we had an unaccounted body in the crematorium.

This can't be right! I thought to myself as I went through the paperwork trying to find an identity for the body in the crematorium. There were no records of any bodies coming in that day. Nor were there any records of any scheduled cremations. So whoever had placed that body there was doing so against protocol. And that was a big problem. I made a mental note right then and there to let my husband know his crew was working against protocol. A mistake like that could have gotten our entire business shut down had the right person seen it.

"This sloppy ass nigga!" I hissed to myself as I hurriedly made my way to the front door. It was my plan to sneak out without Wayne or anyone else ever knowing that I was there. Of course, my plan was cut short when I spotted Trice in the foyer.

"Where the fuck is she at?" she slurred with anger evident in her tone. I looked at her, confused for a moment. I hadn't even seen her, and I had no idea who she was speaking about. Truthfully, I didn't give a fuck. Trice was bad news just like her husband. Normally, whenever she showed up, some type of drunk ass chaos followed behind her.

"Look, I don't know who you're talking about, but there's no one here," I explained in the most calming manner possible.

"Don't give me that bullshit, Shaniece!" Trice barked. I could tell right away that she was past drunk. And for real, I didn't have the time to deal with her shit.

"Look, you need to get the fuck out of here. Every time you

and Choice go through something, you bring the shit to us. This shit is getting old, Trice!" I said seriously and annoyed. I never understood how women could show their ass, knowing that their men were dogs. Like, I could never pop up looking for a man that's not answering my calls. The idea had always seemed foolish to me. If a man wants you, you won't have to look for him. I guess that was something these younger women just didn't understand yet.

"I ain't stupid, Shaniece. I know that he's fucking your new worker. I know he brought her into the side business. Y'all act like a motherfucker is really dumb," she shot back with tears now falling down her face. I tried to piece together the things she was saying, and none of it made sense. But I could tell from the tears and the pain in her voice that she was not making it up. Choice had a female accomplice on our team and I needed to find out who she was and what they were doing.

"Look, go home to your children. When Choice comes here, I will have him call you. You don't need to be out here like this." I tried to console her by sending her on her way. I gently nudged her toward the door as she proceeded to cry her heart out, but she was adamant about meeting this woman.

"I'll go home after you have that bitch come out here!" she said seriously. I could tell from the rage in her eyes she had come there for a fight.

"I already done told you I don't know who you're talking about. You need to go home and stop bringing that shit here every time you and him get into it! You're fucking with my business when you do that. I got a family to feed too!"

"This ain't no damn business. It's a fucking cover-up. And all you motherfuckers are going to go down. Y'all think the joke is on me but really the joke is on you mothafukers!" Trice began to laugh hysterically.

I was just about to get in her ass until I spotted Connor and a couple of his officers approaching us. I looked at her in complete disbelief. Here she was, once again, trying to fuck up my shit because she couldn't keep her man at home.

"Do we have a problem, ladies?" Connor asked happily. He was always eager to report an incident at our funeral home. It's like he had a hard-on for it.

"Yes!" I said matter-of-factly. "This woman has been harassing my staff. She will not leave us alone!"

"Ain't nobody harassing you, bitch!" she replied boldly. "This ain't no regular funeral home and y'all know that. They're smuggling shit and disposing of bodies!" Trice yelled to the police.

"They're moving more dope than the Mexican cartel out of here! You motherfuckers might want to be quiet about it, but I'm not. I'm tired of y'all covering for this nigga. I'm finna blow everybody's fucking cover," Trice continued to scream.

By this time people had started to come outside of the surrounding businesses after hearing a commotion. I lowered my head shamefully as this disrespectful drunk bitch made the biggest scene in front of our establishment. I knew that her goal was to get someone arrested or get the company shut down. Unfortunately, for her, she just didn't have that type of pull.

CHAPTER TWELVE
TRICE

I woke up with another hangover from hell. My head was beating nonstop and it felt like I had literally snorted a cloud and it was now stuck behind my eyes. I was extremely dehydrated and feeling extra drained. I opened my mouth to call for my oldest child and learned that my voice was gone.

"What the fuck?" I said to myself as I tried to think back to what I was doing to lose my voice. Everything seemed to go blank for a minute, and then it all started coming back to me.

"Oh shit! What the fuck did I do that shit for?" I immediately started to scold myself once I remembered what the hell I had done. I knew Choice was going to be mad at me, but I didn't give a fuck. I was sick of him fuckin' on bitches and claiming it was 'business.' Choice had me fucked up. I wasn't about to just lay down and take the punches. I was definitely going to swing back.

"Let me get up and clean this house," I said to myself as I slowly pulled myself out of bed. I figured the least I could do was have the house cleaned and have some food cooked before my husband came home. I was certain it was about to be some drama, but I didn't give a fuck for real. Everyone always played me out to be the crazy person but never took the time to shine light on the reasons behind my actions. I was sick of that. But one thing I couldn't afford was to lose my husband. Drunk me didn't ever think that far she just acted off emotion. Unfortunately, there was nothing I could do about that.

When I finally got downstairs I immediately became discouraged. My kids had completely trashed the house and just looking at it was draining the rest of the little bit of energy I had left inside of me. I figured I'd start with the kitchen so the food could get started while I finished the rest of the house. Before I even had a chance to pick up a wash rag, Choice had come storming into the kitchen.

"You drunk ass bitch!" he screamed as he charged at me. I immediately began to block my face, assuming he was about to hit me. He didn't smack me around like he normally would though. This time he just threw me on the ground.

"You always doing some shit to fuck up my plays. What the fuck is wrong with you? You want a nigga to be broke?" he yelled directly in my face. I tried my hardest to keep my cool because I knew he had a reason to be upset. But the fact that he was screaming at me as if I didn't have a reason to be upset was making that extremely hard to do.

"It's like every time you see me 'bout to win you do something to fuck it up!" he snapped while poking his chest out, like I was one of his opps or something. I didn't flinch because I knew that Choice knew why I was really upset. And he knew me more than anyone else in the world. He wasn't stupid! The problem was, he thought I was stupid!

"See what you're not going to do is play in my face when you know you out here fucking on a whole 'nother bitch." I finally released just a small piece of what was on my mind.

"Ain't nobody fuckin' on no bitches." He lied right to my face before pushing me. I looked at him and shook my head because I knew the reason why he had gotten so upset by my one response was that I was right about my assumptions. Choice was guilty and he knew that I knew it.

"Before you come questioning me about fucking on somebody, you need to make sure you're making yourself fuckable," he barked angrily. I knew that was a direct jab at me. I knew my man better than anybody else knew him. He didn't want to face me. Instead, he wanted to start an argument that I clearly was trying to avoid, all so he could go be with that bitch.

"Ain't nobody stupid, nigga! You trying to start some shit so you can go be with that bitch!" I called him straight out on his bullshit. Ironically, his phone started to ring off the hook. He looked down at it and pretended to be ignoring it because we were arguing. But I knew better and he knew I knew better. That was that bitch calling him.

"For the last time, I'on know who the fuck you talking about. I ain't fuckin' no bitch," he continued on with his lie.

"Okay, so let me see your phone!" I went in for the kill. I knew if that was her calling him, he wasn't going to give up that phone. And, of course, I was right. He looked at me for a moment, completely speechless. I could tell that I had him stick at a crossroad.

"You don't do shit but drink around this motherfucker. The house all fucked up, you ain't cooked or nothing, and all you worried about is checkin' a nigga phone??" he clapped back in a disgusted tone. I knew he was trying to hurt me by the things he was saying. I didn't care though. I knew I wasn't crazy and I couldn't care less 'bout the shit he was saying.

"You want this phone??? Here, go get it!" he added before tossing the phone out of the back door and into the pool. That broke my heart because that let me know for sure that he was hiding more than what I thought. And he had to be crazy to think I wasn't about to go hop in that pool and fish that phone out.

"You that insecure that you about to go jump in a pool for a phone that's already fucked up now?" he asked, obviously trying to belittle me and discourage me from going to the pool. Of course, I didn't care. He had the newest iPhone out and I knew those babies were water resistant. And he knew that too. That's why he was gone by the time I got back inside from retrieving the phone.

CHAPTER THIRTEEN
CHOICE

The moment I saw Trice's crazy ass running toward that pool, I hurried up and jetted to my car. Somehow, some way, that woman always knew when I was doing some shit I had no business doing. I could only pray that that pool had already done some damage to that phone. But with the type of phone I had, I kind of knew that wasn't going to be the case. Trice was going to be hella upset when she saw what was in that phone.

I was low key mad because I didn't want her to even know who Shawnie was or have her number or any of that. I needed Shawnie, she was the key to the exact door that I was trying to open. Trice wasn't going to do anything but fuck that all up. I just couldn't understand that about her. She would constantly fumble bags when she knew she was going to profit off them. She was so jealous that it low key made me hate her. But when it came to Shawnie I definitely understood Trice's frustration. Shawnie wasn't just a regular fling. She was my baby for real. And Trice was right to feel intimidated about her.

Shawnie took me to another place mentally. Trice and I

had been through so much that a part of her would always hate me. I couldn't undo that but I could prevent Shawnie from ever getting to that point. Shawnie didn't bug me or nag at me about shit. She didn't question me 'bout shit, and I knew that was because I hadn't given her a reason not to trust me like I had done with Trice. My mother had always taught me to cherish my wife and never give up on my marriage, but the truth was that I was sick and tired of Trice.

When we first got together Trice was the baddest bitch a man could ask for. She had everything from beauty to brains. Not only was she book smart, she was street smart as well. Trice could do anything from cooking my dope to writing me an affidavit for court. She was just different. She treated me like a king. Trice had that effect where she made me feel like I was the last man on earth. I'm not one of them mushy niggas, but it's something about a woman who makes you feel like she can only see you. Trice was die hard behind me and her love was unconditional, until I started doing bullshit to fuck with her trust. Trice was the greatest person to have on your team but once somebody hurt her, she would become your worst enemy. And that's exactly what was happening with us. Trice was literally going out of her way to fuck up anything I had planned all because she was in her feelings about me fucking with a bitch. And she didn't even know Shawnie, she was just going off her gut feelings. Her showing up to the funeral home like that was way out of line and little did she know, she was literally about to fuck everything up. I couldn't have that. I most definitely couldn't have her running Shawnie off. I had to distance myself from her and FAST.

I hurried to get back to Shawnie's house. I had a feeling that Trice had already talked to her by the time that I pulled up. But saving my relationship with Shawnie was way more important than mending things with Trice. For starters, I knew

Trice would always be in the picture because we had two children together and were married. Trice wasn't bringing me any money or helping me in any way that Shawnie was offering to. And I didn't even have any ties with Shawnie. But I needed them and I was going to get them. And I wasn't about to cut them short for Trice or anybody else.

The moment I got to Shawnie's crib I could tell something was wrong. There was a bag of my clothes that I had been letting pile up there, sitting on the porch. It was funny because I honestly didn't give a damn about materialistic shit. But Shawnie didn't know me well enough to know that. Them clothes would stay outside forever before I picked them up. I cared more about where me and Shawnie stood than I cared about some clothes I could replace on any day.

"Get the fuck off my porch!" she yelled at me through the Ring camera system she had. I could tell from the tone of her voice that she was in her feelings and I knew it was because of Trice's hating ass.

"Please open the door, ma. We need to talk!"

"Go home and talk to your wife."

"It's not what you think! Please open the door and talk to me."

"Fuck you, Choice. I'm not about to let you play games with me. Go find another bitch for that."

"I'm not trying to play with you, Shawnie. I love you, Mama. I don't want to be with that bitch and she knows that, that's why she even hitting you up," I said seriously. I had never told her that I loved her but it felt good to say it and actually mean it. Shawnie made me feel like a kid in middle school again. There was no way I was finna lose her.

"Now you love me." She laughed in a way that let me know she didn't believe me. I didn't care about that though once I heard her unlocking her door.

"Do I look stupid to you?" she asked once we were face to face. She had on one of my tee shirts and her hair was wet. I could tell she was fresh out the shower, and that's when she was the prettiest to me. No makeup, no weave, just Shawnie.

"I can't lose you. I love you," I confessed before grabbing her by her neck and pushing her back into the house. I knew she liked that rough shit and I was finna do everything in my power to please her until I was back in good graces with her.

CHAPTER FOURTEEN
TRICE

"Choice, you need to come home. I didn't have these kids alone and it's not far I gotta sit up playing mommy all day while you're out playing house with bitches." I snapped at my husband. We had been arguing for days about him being in the streets. I mean someone had broke into our home threatening to kill me and our kids over his bullshit and he didn't even care enough to stay home with me.

"I can be out fucking niggas too. We could be taking turns instead just acting like you don't got kids!" I added spitefully.

"Bitch my kids are good. You worried bout fucking somebody when you need to be being a mom and sobering the fuck up." He yelled at me. I started to cry. I hated that he always tried to play me like a drunk when he drank just as much as me and did drugs. On top of that, I needed to drink to even deal with all the bullshit he put me through.

"Is that all you can say?" I yelled irritated with his lack of comebacks. He knew he was dead ass wrong. I was sick and tired of his bullshit. He just didn't have a clue.

"Man get the fuck off my line. Go have a drink!" He said before hanging up on me.

I shook my head at how careless he was. I wanted so badly to hurt that motherfucker but I couldn't think of what to do. I was wore out with life itself and honestly i needed a break from everything. I didn't have anyone to call on, vent to or even get away with. But his ass had a million bitches he could run too. I was about to call him back and flip out on his ass but I decided to make another one instead. A more interesting one.

I took a deep breath before she called the number. For some reason, i was nervous. I'm sure it was because I knew my intentions were wrong. But there was something so inviting about Wayne. I began to relax after the third ring.

'He's not going to answer!' My negative thoughts started to come just as my disappointment started to set in. Then, on the fifth ring he answered.

"Call back and unblock your number!" He said before hanging up the phone.

'CLICK'

Definitely not the answer I was expecting. I smacked my lips at his rather rude demand. 'Who the hell does he think he is?' I thought to myself. I hesitated calling back but another part of me demanded that i follow his command. I called him back with my number unblocked. This time he answered after the first ring.

"Who is this?" Another rude answer.

'Maybe this was a bad idea.' I thought after realizing that being on the phone with him made me freeze up. I didn't even know what I wanted to say to him. I just wanted to talk to him.

"Hello?" He seemed annoyed. I could tell he was about to hang up. I swallowed my negative thoughts and my fears and finally spoke.

"Is this Wayne?" I asked. There was a pause. A very unusual pause. It wasn't awkward though. It was inviting. In a really weird way, it was seductive. Enticing. It made me instantly want more of him.

"Who is this?" He asked.

"Who do you want it to be?" I threw out a candy coated pass. I figured if I flirted minimally, I'd have an idea of just how far I could go with him. I bit my lips as if he was right in front of me waiting on his reply.

"Trice!" The way he said my name weakened me. I couldn't describe the feeling it gave me, but I liked it.

"How'd you know it was me?" I asked seriously.

"I didn't. You asked who I wanted it to be and I answered you." There was another pause. This time the pause was brief. Still, it was alluring to me.

"Damn, it's been two weeks. Why you just now calling?"

"I got bored." I laughed.

"You got bored?" He paused again. I could tell he was smiling.

"Where you at, girl?"

"I'm about to leave work."

"I want to see you." He almost sounded like he was begging me. She liked it and wasted no time responding.

"I'm going to go home and change. I'll call you in an hour or so."

"Nah, call me at seven!" He ordered me. Everyone who knew me knew that she wasn't okay with taking orders, but it felt okay coming from him. I loved when a man could take control and I was definitely trying to see more of him.

"I'll call you at seven." I replied obediently.

"Make sure you clear your schedule tonight. I don't like being rushed."

"I'll be ready." I assured him before hanging up the phone and melting into my seat like a middle school girl who had just found her first crush. I was starting to see more and more everyday that I should've picked the daddy and not the damn son.

CHAPTER FIFTEEN
SHAWNIE

The sun beaming through the window gently tugged me out of the deep sleep I had fallen into. It felt so good to wake up snuggled in a man's arms. Of course, it was bittersweet being that it was Choice's arms. I could tell from the way he held me that he was seriously falling in love with me, and I didn't want that. I was only around him for one reason and it had nothing to do with his heart.

I slowly slid from his embrace, careful not to wake him up. I knew the second he got up, he was going to be all over me and I didn't need that. See, I didn't give a damn about Choice for real. It was all an act for my job. Being a cop wasn't easy.

Sometimes, my job requires me to go undercover and make people fall in love with me. I mean, my boss has never told me to go out and fuck a perp, but I had my own way of operating. Hell, this case wasn't even assigned to me. I was just looking for my son, Trell. He wasn't an angel but he was my son. He had been missing for over three months and no one seemed to care anymore.

For starters, I am a well-respected federal agent with more

than fifteen years on the force. When my son first disappeared, every cop and agent was out looking for him. We had the best of the best investigators and detectives looking for Trell. We just couldn't seem to find him. After about three weeks, everyone slowly decided to lose hope. My boss was saying we were putting in too much time trying to find Trell.

"I'm sorry. We just don't have the money," he had said to me after telling me the search was being called off.

That devastated me completely because I knew my son was out there somewhere. And as a mother I simply couldn't give up on finding him. I continued passing out flyers and going to interview people. One day I was walking in a neighborhood that my son used to hang out at when a homeless woman approached me. The woman was clearly high off something and smelled as if she hadn't ever showered in her life.

"Your son was cremated," she said to me. I looked at her, confused about what the hell made her say that. I was about to ask her but before I got the chance to, she was already answering me.

"That's what happens to all the missing people. They're murdered on the street and then this funeral home called Wettler's gets paid to dispose of the body. Everyone on the streets is talking about it. The cops just don't seem to care," she explained to me. I had heard a thing or two about Wettler's Funeral Home but not anything as serious as disposing of a body. They were suspected of drug smuggling and money laundering and now they were on my radar.

I started by staking out the funeral home for a few days. I noticed a local drug dealer by the name of Quan. He didn't know who I was so I approached him when I saw him exiting the funeral home.

"Do you work here?" I asked as if I didn't know who he was.

"Nah, this my homeboy family business. I'm just visiting," he explained to me.

"Okay, I'm trying to get an estimate on a funeral. I'll just go inside," I lied. Quan obviously didn't know what I was on. He just smiled and licked his lips as he watched me switch off. On my way inside the funeral home, I noticed a Ryders van. Ryders was a transportation service that brought bodies from the coroners to the funeral homes. After checking to make sure no one was inside or close by, I snatched a jacket from the front seat and put it on. I was determined to get inside that funeral home and look around for any clues about Trell. That's when I met Choice and I could tell from the moment he saw me, I could easily have him eating out the palm of my hand.

"I wouldn't have you riding around dropping off dead people if you were my girl," he said to me after noticing the Ryders jacket I was wearing. I smiled gently and pretended to be going on about my business.

"Hold on one second, let me holla at you."

"I'm not interested in dating. I'm just here to make my money and go home," I responded seriously. I had to stand my ground and make him work a lil' harder.

"Shit, I'm trying to make some money too. And for real, we can work together. I'll make you a few extra thousand a week and all you would have to do is work your same job and just make a couple extra stops for me," he said matter-of-factly. I knew right away it was some illegal shit, but I was okay with that because it would get me closer to finding out what happened to my son and give me more ammo when it was time to light Choice's ass up and throw him under a cell.

CHAPTER SIXTEEN
WAYNE

"Hello, is this Dwayne?" an unfamiliar voice spoke to me after I answered my phone. I looked at the number, hoping that would help me catch the voice. But it didn't. I didn't recognize the number or the voice for the life of me.

"This is Dwayne, may I ask who is calling?" I asked with the most polite voice I could muster. I didn't know who was on my line and if it was somebody important, I damn sure didn't want to be rude.

"This is Ron Stanley with Messer and Company."

"Who?" I asked, confused about what the hell he was trying to say to me.

"We're working on your The Wettler's bar and restaurant for you. And we just finished it up," Ron said, refreshing my memory. I had bought some land across the street from Wettler's a couple years back. I hadn't told my wife, but I was planning on it becoming an extension to the funeral home. We were making so much money off funerals that being able to host the repast was almost kind of mandatory. It didn't make sense for us not to.

See, Wettler's wasn't my company. Shaniece's family had left that business to her. But me being her husband, I had helped her and dedicated a big part of my life to keeping this thing going. I always felt like the business was the foundation to our happiness, but I also felt threatened by the fact that it wasn't mine. I knew that Shaniece could up and leave whenever she wanted and take the family business with her. So in a sense, that meant my own happiness wasn't mine. And I simply couldn't stand for that.

Now, I loved my wife but I loved money more. Shaniece had always been my ticket out but even if it weren't for her, I would've made some shit shake. That's just who I am. I'm not a buster, a sucker, or none of that. I'm a real nigga and I get to the paper by any means. I'm not a user. I don't depend on my woman but if she got it, I definitely needed some of it. If that makes sense!

The moment I got into business with her, I was in awe of how much money was coming in and out of that place. I knew my wife was paid but she never reported exactly how paid she was to me. Hell, she didn't even report it to the IRS. Not fully anyway. When I saw how much potential was in that place, I knew that I was set for life. I just had to find a way to tap into that flow permanently. And that's exactly what I did.

I started off by helping some of my homeboys who were still slanging dope in the street. They needed a safe way to smuggle their dope from one place to another. I knew that with a legal transportation vehicle, no one would suspect us for doing any wrong. Nine times out of ten, the police wouldn't even bother us. I quickly came up with a way to smuggle any and everything I could.

Every week when we got our scheduling, I'd report to them

where we had to drop bodies off. Sometimes it would be local, out of town, or even out of state. If they needed to get something there or close to there, they would send money and drop the product off. I'd then have my medical examiner tuck off the drugs in one of the bodies so that no one involved was aware of what's going on. Not the driver, not the other morgues and funeral homes. Nobody but me, my client, and my medical examiner. Of course, she had the authority to enter any morgue or funeral home. It was then she would extract the drugs and safely deliver them without not issues.

Life seemed to be going great until my son Choice started bringing on heat. I couldn't tell what he was doing to bring the heat, but I knew it was him. He was threatening our entire company with his careless and immature actions. I had even heard rumors on the street that he was disposing bodies for $10,000. I never caught him but I had a feeling there was some type of truth to it just from how the police were pressuring me. That's why I built the bar and restaurant across the street. That would allow me to completely cancel out my side business without canceling out my cash flow. And it secured my cash flow in case Shaniece ever did get fed up enough to leave, because the restaurant was in my name. It was a win-win situation for me.

All I had to do now was butter my wife up and make her excited about the restaurant. And I knew exactly how to do that. I was about to wake her up to breakfast in bed, dick her down real quick, and surprise her with the restaurant.

CHAPTER SEVENTEEN
SHANIECE

"Baby," I heard my husband calling me out of my sleep. I was so worn out from trying to manage everything we had going on that I hadn't even had any time to relax. I had literally been getting about two to three hours of sleep every night for like the past month. Today was the first day I had where I actually got to sleep in, and here was my husband waking me up.

"Get up, baby," he called out for me again. I tried my hardest to stay sleep but the truth was once I got disturbed out of my sleep, I couldn't go back. No matter how long I stayed in bed. Once I was up, I was up.

"Good afternoon, baby!" Dwayne said cheerfully once he saw I was waking up.

"What's going on?" I asked, confused about why he was even waking me up.

"I have a surprise for you," he said cheerfully.

"Oh god, what you done did now?" I asked while slowly lifting up in the bed. I knew my husband good and well. He wasn't the type to just do nice things for me out of the blue.

Maybe for Vera but definitely not for me. I knew better than anyone that Dwayne had something up his sleeve.

"I haven't done anything. I just been feeling so distant from you. And I want you to know you're still the closest thing to my heart," he added, gently placing a kiss on my forehead.

"I got you breakfast!" he told me as he spun around and grabbed a silver tray off my dresser. The tray had a ton of fruits and raw veggies on it. Just the way I liked it. He knew me all too well because one thing I didn't believe was that I should be eating pig butt and aborted chickens for breakfast.

"I made you a smoothie too!" he added while placing the tray on my bed. I immediately started eating the food. I was more than halfway through when I noticed there was a small gift box on the tray.

"What's this?" I asked curiously. I was almost positive that it was a ring based off the shape and size of the box. What was confusing me was the fact that he was suddenly being the perfect husband again.

"Open it," he said happily.

I opened the box and was immediately melted by the sight of the Diamond Dahlia Flower Fashion Ring inside the box. It was a ring I had been looking at. I had even cut it out the magazine and put it on my refrigerator. It was a gift I was already going to buy myself. It cost a whopping five thousand dollars, but I'm telling you it was worth every penny. It was the type of ring to make you fall in love all over again.

"Oh baby, you got it!" I cooed as I jumped into his arms. "Thank you so much!" I was damn near in tears.

"That's just a promise ring. I wanted to let you know I appreciate you and remind you of my promise to always do better for us."

"It's beautiful," I confessed. I allowed myself to melt in his embrace. I didn't do that much because I didn't really trust him anymore. I felt like he was using me at times or cheating on me at other times. Still, in that moment, I was reminded that he was my husband and I loved him.

"I got something better for you too," he added proudly. I seriously couldn't think of anything else he could have done that would be better than what he had already done for me.

"Just get dressed and meet me in the car," he said to me before exiting the room.

I jumped up out that bed so fast and flew into my bathroom. I hurried to shower and toss on a sundress. Sundresses were always my go to. Especially when I didn't have time to pick out an outfit. I found an all-white sundress then threw on a jean jacket and some white sandals before I could even lotion myself up. I quickly added my jewelry and a little perfume before rushing out the house.

I got inside the car and relaxed into the seat. I loved the way his car smelled. It was a mixture of the finest weed and the finest cologne and a hint of money. The smell alone made me want to hop all over him. It was so hard for me to stay in my own seat and not force myself on him.

My whole mind drew a blank when I realized he was taking me to funeral home. I was so confused, because what the hell could be so special about a place I saw every mother fucking day?

"Dwayne, what's going on? Why are we here?" I asked, confused.

"You're looking in the wrong place." He smiled, nodding his head across the street. I followed his eyes to the newly constructed building across the street. I had watched them build it but never paid no mind to it until today.

"Why is my family's name on that building?" I asked, confused.

"I told you I was going to always make us better, right?" he asked seriously.

"Yes, please tell me what's going on," I begged eagerly.

"This will be our repast center. It has lounging areas, bathrooms, a full bar, and a full restaurant. It's the perfect extension and it gives me a reason to keep everyone out of your way. There's no way we won't win with this, baby," he said to me just as we exited the car to go check out the inside.

CHAPTER EIGHTEEN
CHOSEN

"Come on, ma! I ain't trying to be in here all day," I told Vera as I impatiently waited on her to finish finding something to wear to the grand opening of The Wettler's Repast Center. I hated being out in public places, simply because I could never have full control. I never wanted to be in a place I couldn't run my way, if things went left. Hell, I hated for Vera to be out in public. She most definitely couldn't ever go in public alone. Anytime she wanted to step out, I personally made sure she was either with me or someone in the family.

"How am I supposed to pick out a cute outfit with you rushing me like this all the time?" she snapped back with her hands on her thick ass hips. Her neck was rolling and I wasn't even listening to what she was saying anymore. I was just stuck on how beautiful she was. I loved that woman and it was like I literally fell deeper for her every day.

"You could've picked out a cute outfit at home," I replied in a joking manner. I knew she would know I was referring to the many brand-new outfits she had sitting in her closet.

She immediately sucked her teeth and rolled her eyes at me. We both began to laugh. She couldn't even say anything because she knew I was telling the truth. Vera was the most spoiled woman I knew. She was just humble with her shit. And bad as ever. That was one of the main things I loved about Vera. She couldn't be less than perfect on any scale.

The sound of my phone ringing snatched me out of the daze staring at Vera had thrown me into. She turned to me and rolled her eyes again. This time to place emphasis on how much she hated my phone taking me away from her. She never had to worry about another woman or anything like that, but sometimes business would call and I would have no choice but to leave her. I signaled for her to go on with her shopping as I stepped outside to take my call.

"Chosen, where the fuck are you?" It was my father. And from the tone of his voice, he was pissed the hell off.

"I'm out with Vera. What's going on?"

"I need you and your brother to get down here to my office as soon as possible. Shaniece just told me about the police trying to storm our shit again. All over Choice and Trice's bullshit." My dad started to rant faster than I could process.

"Choice and Trice?" I asked, confused. My brother somehow always managed to end up in the center of all the bullshit. I simply couldn't understand the shit.

"What this nigga done did now?" I asked with a chuckle, just imagining what the hell he was up to now.

"Nah, this shit not even funny. He's doing all types of bullshit on the side in the streets and that bitch Trice is shining a light on it. We gotta fix this shit ASAP or we're all at risk of going down for his shit!" my father said seriously.

"Ok, I'll be there in a minute, Pops," I explained to him before hanging up the call. I turned to go let Vera know that she really needed to put a rush on it. Just as I was about to step back inside the store, a group of four men approached me.

"What's up, lil' nigga," one of them said. I looked at them, confused by the aggression in the dude's tone. In addition to that, I hadn't ever seen either one of them before. But from the looks of it, they all were the little niggas. And some little broke niggas at that.

"Little?" I asked, unsure if they really wanted to try to 'lil' nigga' me.

"Ain't that what the fuck he just said?" another one of them asked while shoulder bumping me.

"What's going on?" Vera came running out of the store. I could tell by the tone of her voice that she was afraid, and that pissed me off.

"This nigga and his brother covered up my cousin's murder," the first guy told Vera.

"What?" I was completely lost as to who these guys were or what they were talking about, but I was sure that they had the wrong guy. "Listen, y'all got me mixed up with somebody else," I started to explain before the second guy rudely interrupted me again.

"Nigga, we know who the fuck you are. You and your brother burning bodies in that funeral home and bragging about it," he said seriously. My mind immediately went to the call I had just took from my father. Now I had a better idea of why he was as mad as he was.

"We know that's what happened to T-Baby and it's time to answer for that shit," the first guy hopped back in.

"Man, y'all niggas better get the fuck up out my way before this shit get tragic!" I warned them, but they didn't want to listen. Before I could get anything else out, one of them hit me.

The hit was soft as hell. Dude didn't even faze me. I immediately got on his ass. His boys were so stunned by my handwork that I got at least a good ten punches in on their boy before they even started jumping in.

They all rushed at me but they weren't tough enough to get me down. I was flinging them boys around and dropping they asses one by one, over and over. Everything was going smooth until I saw Vera jump into the fight.

"Get the fuck off my man!" she hissed as she started socking everybody coming at me.

"Mind yo' business, bitch!" I heard one of them say before punching Vera in the face. She fell to the ground, immediately losing consciousness. That was enough to send me into a rage.

"Y'all got me fucked up!" I yelled before removing my gun off my waistline.

"Oh shit, he got a gun!" one of the men hurried to alert his crew, but they were too late. I already had perfect shots on all of them.

"I told y'all motherfuckers this shit was going to get tragic!" I reminded them about my warning to them before I started shooting them one by one.

CHAPTER NINETEEN
VERA

"Ma'am? Are you alright?" a paramedic asked me the moment I opened my eyes. My head was spinning and I couldn't for the life of me remember where I was or what had happened.

"How many fingers am I holding up?" the paramedic asked while waving four fingers in front of my face. I looked at him like he was four different types of crazy. I lifted up off the floor in hopes of getting a better perception of what was going on. Then suddenly and all at once, I could hear everything around me. There were people screaming, children crying, and a ton of whispers through the crowd.

"That dude put her to sleep," I heard someone whisper. I looked around, still not able to remember what happened. I noticed I was in the mall and my memory slowly started coming back.

"Chosen!" I screamed once I remembered that I got knocked out while trying to fight men off him.

"Hey, calm down!" the paramedic told me as he restrained me from trying to jump up.

"Where the fuck is my man?" I snapped. I looked around to see three of the four man that had started the fight with him stretched out on the floor. Two of them were covered in sheets already and the last one was still fighting for his life.

"Where the fuck is my man!" I yelled again. I knew he wouldn't have left me there and I was afraid something had happened to him after I passed out.

"Your 'man' has been arrested for two counts of murder and one attempted murder!" I heard a voice call out from behind me. I turned around to face him and was disgusted to see it was Detective Randolph. He had been harassing our family for about a year and I could tell he was just loving this.

"How the hell you going to arrest him when them mother-fuckers started shit with us?? Chosen was just defending us!" I yelled in his defense.

"Well, if he was just defending you all then he has nothing to worry about!" Detective Randolph replied sarcastically.

"Let's get you to the hospital!" the paramedic spoke before I had a chance to respond to Detective Randolph.

"Fuck that! I'm going to go get my man!" I hissed as I jumped up off the floor. I took off running as fast as I could to make it to my car. I kept replaying my aunt's suspicions in my head. She had been trying to warn Uncle Wayne for years about Choice's actions coming back one day to bite us in the ass. Now I understood exactly what she was scared of. Only difference was it was happening to my man and not hers. I had to get to my aunt and uncle Wayne and let them know what was going on with Chosen.

"Aunt Shaniece!" I screamed the moment I busted through her office door.

"What's wrong?" my uncle Wayne screamed the second he heard panic in my voice.

"Where is Chosen at?" my aunt asked after noticing he

hadn't run in behind me.

"They took him!" I said as I dropped down to my knees in tears.

"What do you mean they took him?" Uncle Wayne asked, confused. "Who took him?" he added, clearly in search of answers.

"The police!" I cried.

"The police? What happened. Vera, tell us what's going on!" my aunt pleaded.

"We were at the mall when this group of guys approached us. They said that Choice had been bragging about burning their cousin's body. Chosen tried to tell them that he had nothing to do with what they were talking about but a fight broke out," I explained.

"And then what?" Uncle Wayne asked, now even more concerned about his son than before.

"One of them put me to sleep and when I woke up, two of them were dead and another was fighting for his life still. I don't know what happened to the fourth one."

"And Chosen?" Uncle Wayne inquired.

"Detective Randolph told me he was being charged with murder and attempted murder. We have got to go get him out of there."

"Oh my god. That little boy!" my aunt Shaniece thought out loud. Me and uncle Wayne both looked at her confused.

"What little boy?" Uncle Wayne questioned her.

"There was a boy here a couple months ago. He was in the crematorium and he was unidentified. I had a bad feeling about it and now I understand why," Aunt Shaniece said with a tone that suggested that her heart was broken. I knew how she felt about family and I knew how much she respected her company. She was devastated when she realized exactly what was going on in her company behind closed doors.

CHAPTER TWENTY
SHANIECE

I tried my hardest not to blow a gasket. I was so upset that it was literally taking everything in me not to start flipping out on my husband. I had been telling him over and over that his son was up to no good, and he didn't want to listen to me. Now, not only was I under fire but my family's legacy was too. I couldn't stop thinking about that little boy I saw laying on that table. I knew for sure he wasn't supposed to be there. I felt it in my bones. But I would've never guessed that his murder was being covered up. Still, I can't lie, something definitely didn't feel right when I first saw him.

"We have got to clean this place up real good," I told my husband. I had a feeling the cops were on their way in and I wasn't about to take any chances with Choice doing stupid shit like that. "No wonder the goddamn police are on our ass, because your son is out here doing stupid shit like this!" I yelled at Dwayne.

"Calm down, Shaniece!" he snapped at me. I knew he was frustrated behind his son's actions too, but I didn't give a fuck. He was about to have to hear my mouth.

"Calm down?? This is my family legacy on the line. That lil' boy was somebody's baby. Does that sound like some shit I need to be being calm about?? Your other son is facing a double homicide because of him! What the fuck is your problem?" I yelled at him. I hated how he always tried to baby Choice. I knew that was his baby, but god damn. Dwayne was acting like he was sucking Choice's dick or something. I just couldn't understand the shit and I was tired of it. Enough was enough.

"All I'm saying is that you need to chill. Ain't nothing going to get done if we just stand here and holler at each other. I understand you were right, baby. I apologize. Now let me fix it."

"And how are you going to do that?"

"I'll hire cleaners to come clean the place brand new. We will throw out everything at an unknown location. We refund every customer for the next two days, postpone the grand opening, and get this motherfucker exactly the way you like it," he assured me, but I couldn't accept his promises. Not that easy and definitely not with him being so nonchalant about the shit.

"You don't think the police are on their way?" I asked, confused as to why he was playing like he didn't understand how the streets worked.

"Listen, all I need you to do is ride with Vera and get Chosen. Please just let me handle everything else," he said in a tone that I felt was way too calm.

"Yes Auntie, can we please just listen to him!" Shaniece begged. She sounded like she was agreeing with him, but I knew she was only in agreement because he had said for us to go get Chosen. That kind of pissed me off even more because I felt like everybody there only cared about what they had going on. No one seemed to care about my feelings or my family's business that was on the fucking line.

"You better fix this shit!" I hissed one last time before grabbing my keys and heading for the door.

"I got you, baby!" Wayne promised me. "And after this, I promise Choice won't ever be able to step foot inside this bitch again!" he added before walking Vera and myself to the door.

CHAPTER TWENTY-ONE
CHOSEN

"Trays!!" I heard one of the guards announce just before eight p.m. I instantly became irritated upon realizing that I was still in jail. The judge had given me a bond earlier that morning and I simply couldn't understand what was taking Vera so long.

Man, my baby better not be hurt! A piece of me started to panic as my thoughts began to race. The last time I checked, Vera was on the ground. And everything was so out of control that I didn't even get the chance to rush to her side. I literally had to start killing niggas off and before I could make it to her, the police had me.

Naturally, I started to think of every worst-case scenario imaginable. I loved the fuck out of Vera. She was literally the apple of my eye, and I was going to burn the whole fucking city down if something had happened to her after them punk ass cops came. They called themselves roughing me up. They threw a couple punches, hit me with their club sticks, and maced me. But I ate all of that shit!

I hated those motherfuckers just as much as I hated the

thought of losing Vera. I hadn't even done anything wrong at the mall and here they were fucking with me. All I was doing was defending myself and my girl. And I would've done that without killing nobody, had dude not started punching on Vera. That was a big no-no. They had to think I was soft or something. They for damn sure hadn't done their homework or they would've known not to try that shit with me. I would do life over that shit any fucking day. I didn't mind sitting in jail over defending myself or my girl. My problem was that all of this shit had happened behind Choice's ass. That nigga had me fucked up and he definitely was going to have to answer to me about that shit!

"I got next on this phone!" I told the line of bum ass niggas at the phone how the line was about to go. A couple of them looked at me funny but I didn't give a fuck. I was on whatever they was on and my body language said that and more.

"Y'all niggas got a problem with that?" I asked, confused about what all the murmuring and side glares they started doing was about.

"Yea, I got a problem with that shit, G!" A tall, cocky-looking motherfucker decided to step to me. I smiled with excitement. See, I was a firm believer that God would sometimes put targets in your way. People who intentionally jump in your line of fire while you're going through what you're going through. This big, bulky ass nigga decided to stick his head in my business when he wasn't even in the phone line. Shit had nothing to do with him at all.

I waited patiently on him to get close to me. He was walking up to me, talking all tough while wrapping up his hand with a ripped-up shirt. I don't know what made his ass think that was gone faze me, because it didn't. Not even a little bit.

He laughed. Two nearby peons started to laugh with him before deciding to join him on his walk toward me.

"If I was y'all niggas, I would take my ass back over to my bunk so I don't get embarrassed in front of the entire dorm," I said seriously to him.

"Yea, see, now that's where you're wrong!" the big bulky guy replied with an almost demonic smile. But that smile didn't faze me. I knew there was way more demon in my blood than in his.

Almost as if on cue, one of the guys on the phone hung up. I looked at the guy next in line to see if he was gone challenge me as I walked to grab the phone. He didn't. He just let me grab it. I nodded my head as a lil' way of saying thank you before I started to dial Choice's phone number. That motherfucker had me fucked up and he definitely was about to hear about it.

As soon as I dialed the number and the phone started to ring, Mr. Bulky sent one of his lil' peons over to hang up my phone call. I couldn't believe that shit for real. Like who the hell did they think they were?

I immediately grabbed the dude by the throat and started beating his face in with the phone. Mr. Bulky sent his second peon over to help. I dropped dude with one punch and then twisted the wire from the phone around his neck.

"Y'all niggas really tryna die over a phone call?" I asked as I strangled the life out of the peon. I kept my foot on the other one's neck so that he was unable to move. Within thirty seconds both of them soft ass men were tapping on the floor, begging me to let them go.

I removed my grip from the second guy's neck and then my foot from the first guy's. They both got up and ran away from me. The bulky leader looked at me confused like he hadn't ever seen a fight before. I could tell he didn't want any smoke, but a part of him was acting like he wasn't ready to back down.

"Don't piss me off in here!" I warned him before redialing Choice's phone number. That's who I was really mad at, not Mr. Bulky or his peons, but since they wanted parts I gave it to them.

"What's the word?" Choice answered the phone like there wasn't absolutely anything wrong.

"What's the word??" I asked, offended by his too cool for TV response. "Bro, are you smoking dick or something?" I couldn't think of anything else that would make him act so damn stupid.

"Chill, I heard what happened bro, we're gonna fix it."

"Man, get me the fuck out of here, today!" I barked.

"Dad already sent Vera and Shaniece. Just chill. You know we not finna leave you in there."

"Motherfucker, you need to take your own advice and chill. Then maybe I wouldn't even be here," I snapped. I couldn't believe how this nigga just played innocent like he ain't have shit to do with nothing.

"I told you I'ma handle it," he said in a tone that suggested I was getting on his nerves.

"Bitch ass nigga, you should've been handled that shit. The shit should've never happened. Got me locked up away from my bitch. Niggas hitting her and shit. Nigga, you obviously don't got no control over this shit," I confessed.

"Bro, not on the phone, man. We gone talk in person," he said sarcastically like he was some big-time dope dealer. That motherfucker was as dumb as they came. He should've known how to relay his message to me without saying too much, but no. He couldn't seem to do shit but bring more trouble people's way. Fed up with his bullshit and not willing to feed into his fairytale life, I decided to hang up the phone. Not even five seconds after that they were calling me to pack up my things. I couldn't help but to smile. I was so happy to be going back home that it was kind of pathetic.

"Now y'all niggas can have the phone!" I said out of spite as I threw that bitch on the ground and started packing my bed and things up.

CHAPTER TWENTY-TWO
SHAWNIE

I smiled gracefully as my son entered the kitchen. His skin was glowing and his hair was freshly cornrowed and lace stitched to perfection. His jewelry was blinging as usual. My baby always did his thing. He didn't dress like a thug or none of that. He was a boss and he conducted himself as such.

Most boys his age wanted to be like rappers but my son wanted to be like Frank Lucas until he found out Lucas snitched. Still, that was his idol. His favorite movie was American Gangster. He would watch that movie every single day, even as an adult. I knew he was taking notes. I watched him conduct himself every day like that man. I knew there was no saving him from experiencing a lifestyle that he was born obsessed with. All I could do was try to teach him along the way and hope he'd get his taste and get out. But knowing who his father was, I knew that wasn't an option.

My son was doomed from birth, simply because of who his father was. He had that gangster shit in his blood. It ran through his veins and pumped out of his heart. My baby's father, Latrell Martin, was one of the most notorious gangsters to ever roam the streets of Diego.

I originally met him as a teenager in high school. We didn't go to a public school and we weren't living in the ghetto. Still, he was wild as hell. He had to be the toughest boy in the school and I fell head over heels for him. Instantly too!

Later, I learned that he was actually a kid from the ghetto who got placed in foster care. When I asked him about it, he told me his family had been murdered in front of him and as a result, he was a ward of the state. From that moment forward, I vowed to always be in his life. I promised him I would always love him and I would always be his family.

Before I was eighteen, Latrell had already gotten me pregnant. My mother and father were so disappointed to find out that they literally packed me up and moved me away. That didn't surprise me though. My parents lived their entire lives with sticks up their ass. I already knew they would try to ship me off and maybe even kill my baby. That's why I made sure to hide my pregnancy until I was too far along for anybody's abortion. And by the time my son was born, I was eighteen.

My entire life went to shambles when my family took me away from Latrell. I tried to go back and find him but he was gone. I kept praying and praying to find him but it never worked out. After a while, I started to focus less on Latrell and more on our junior.

My son became my entire life. He was all I had of Latrell and I literally worshipped that baby. I knew I had to make a good life for him so he would never be in his father's shoes. I went to college, graduated, and went straight to the police academy. I had wanted to be a cop since I was a child. I loved cop shows and other shows of that nature. I told myself I wasn't going to stop until I got there. I had to set a good example for my son and that's what I did.

I never gave any man the time of day again. I never dated anyone or even cared to meet new people. I had that type of entertainment on the job and it literally restricted me from catching feelings for a motherfucker. Anytime I'd get horny or want some affection, I'd get it from a perp. It was my little way of using what I had to get what I wanted. I could get my nut off with no commitments and I could crack my case while doing it.

My secret was I never revealed myself to the men I took down, never stood in court, and never gave them my real name. So even when they saw my name on that paperwork they didn't know who I was. Hell, some of them I would even pay my little cousins to keep in touch with through mail until sentencing. As a result, they never thought to mention to their lawyers that they had been fucking on the lead detective on the case. That method was working perfectly until I was handed my first big case.

The name of the perp was Scar. He was a big-time drug dealer who was smuggling more drugs than a little bit. He was believed to be one of the biggest suppliers on the West Coast. He owned mansions, yachts, jets, the whole nine. And because he was so well off, he was being investigated for money laundering. In addition to that, police suspected him of orchestrating murders. Literally anybody who stood up to that man or agreed to go against him in court went missing.

When my boss was explaining the case to me, I remember thinking, damn, that's one bad motherfucker. Then I saw the picture and nearly fainted. It was Latrell. My son's dad had grown up to be a millionaire gangster who went by the name of Scar. It was bittersweet. I wanted so bad to be around him but I knew he was under fire. Still, I loved him enough to use where I was in life to get us both were we needed to be.

After taking the job, I went to go see him. I told him from

jump exactly what was going on and helped him clean up his case by intentionally framing his partners or getting rid of certain charges. I made sure I told Scar how to move, made a couple calls, and just like that, I had my family back. My son had his father and I still had my job.

Unfortunately, Scar had done entirely too much to get off completely scot free. He ended up getting shipped off to do eight years in prison. He left me with a few million dollars to set me and keep my son straight. I promised to wait for him and keep it low key while he was away. That was the only reason I even worked, aside from my own dirty desires my job fulfilled. I continued to live like a bum instead of the millionaire I was, being careful not to alarm the wrong people.

"I love you more, momma!" were Scar's last words to me before they locked him away. And ironically, they were my son's last words to me before he was killed.

He had come into the kitchen and sat at the table. I was making breakfast and listening to CNN.

"Good morning, where you on your way to?" I asked after noticing that he was fully dressed in one of his immaculate suits.

"I got a little play on this money!" he told me before flashing me his father's smile. I immediately got an eerie feeling in my gut. I always worried about him. I didn't want my son dying trying to get money we already had. Yet, I couldn't tell him about it because then I would be risking everything me and his father were working toward.

"Money ain't everything!" I told him as I placed a breakfast sandwich in front of him.

"Yea, but we damn sure can't live without it." He smirked before grabbing his sandwich and kissing me on the cheek.

"I love you, Son," I told him seriously.

"I love you more, Momma." And just like that, he was gone and I was awakened from the same dream that I have every single night. Forced to face the harsh reality that my son was really dead. And here I was, in bed with one of the men who had something to do with his murder.

CHAPTER TWENTY-THREE

CHOICE

"What's the matter, babe?" I asked, confused as to why Shawnie was pushing herself away from me in her sleep. I hated when she did that shit. It made me feel like she was sleeping with another man or something. It was almost like she wasn't expecting to see me when she woke up. The shit confused the hell out of me each time, because it's like who the fuck are you expecting?

Of course, I never said nothing to crazy to her about it because I didn't want to sound like a lunatic. Shawnie had been with me every single night. She went to work at her lil' call center job and came straight home to me. Hell, I hadn't even been home to Trice in about three months. Shawnie was basically my girl now and she couldn't breathe without me hearing it. I had every intention on spending the rest of my life with her. Once I had Trice all the way out of the picture, Shawnie and I were going to run off into the sunset how the white folks do in the movies.

Trice wasn't going willingly, of course! She had made my life a living hell since the day I told her we were done. I hadn't seen my kids and sadly, I had accepted that I may never see them until they were grown. I didn't care though. That wasn't enough to make me stay away from Shawnie. I wanted the real thing. I mean, what I shared with Trice was real, but it was too damaged. I didn't have the desire to even try to fix it. Besides, I knew I could have that and more with Shawnie. Hell, I could even have more children with her.

There was literally nothing Trice could do that Shawnie couldn't. She was beautiful and she always made sure a nigga ate. She washed my clothes, kept the house clean, and even helped me out with organizing my money moves. Anything I did, she was right by my side.

Shawnie was a rider for real and she didn't need a drink to ride. It was just natural. I could tell that whoever she was with had taught her something, and I was certain they were dying to have her back. And that's exactly what they were going to have to do to try and get her back, because I was going to kill about her. She was the one I wasn't going to play any games with or play any games about. Shawnie was mine now. And nothing was ever going to change that.

"Oh, I'm sorry baby!" Shawnie apologized after fully waking up out of her sleep and realizing that she was pushing me off her once again.

"Yea, what's that shit about? What you thinking about another nigga or something?" I asked seriously but in a joking manner. I wasn't about to let nobody play with my feelings and I think a piece of Shawnie knew that.

"Actually, I was dreaming about my son," she said rudely. I immediately began to scold myself for even pushing that button. Anytime it came to her son, Shawnie overdid it. I mean, I'd imagine it's hard to lose a son but she just over did it. I hated hearing about that shit. It always ruined the mood. She'd get all upset and stay that way for the entire day. The sad part about it was I was almost certain that I had cremated her son. Unfortunately, there had just been so many bodies that I never cared to look at them, let alone remember them. But with the way the city was, I knew for sure that she would never get her son back.

"Baby, you know I was joking." I lied as I wrapped my arms around her. I at least wanted to be able to comfort her since I believed I played a role in her pain. I wondered how she would look at me if she knew the type of things I was really into. But that didn't matter because she would never find out. I was making so much money from the smuggling gigs with her that she wouldn't even notice there were any other streams of income. As long as I could keep that a secret from her, we were going to be good.

"I'm going to go shower!" She replied in a tone that made me feel like now she had an attitude.

"Shawnie, please!" I attempted to calm her but my attempt was interrupted by the sound of my phone ringing. She took that as her cue to scurry off to the bathroom. I decided to answer my phone instead of chasing after her.

"You need to fix this shit!" It was my dad and he was obviously upset. That didn't even surprise me because he always seemed to be upset with me. Everybody was.

"Man I don't know what everybody talking about, Dad. I wouldn't do no shit like that!" I lied to him. I knew he knew I was erasing bodies but I couldn't admit it to him. I didn't understand why it even mattered to him with all the illegal bullshit his ass was into.

"Ain't that many people lying on you." He he hissed. The anger was so strong in his voice that I thought he was going to hop through the phone on me. "You gone have to get the fuck up out of here and take that bitch with you. You're not finna fuck up what me and my wife done built."

"You mean what her family built?" I challenged him. I couldn't believe he was talking to me like he could exile me or something. He definitely had me fucked up.

"I mean what the fuck YOU didn't build. Don't fucking play with me, boy. I will fuck you up and you know it."

"I'm not trying to disrespect you, Dad." I decided to throw in the towel. I needed to be in good graces with him because I wasn't trying to lose my side business with Raj. In a sense, I needed access to Wettler's in order to be able to keep my plan in motion. I had a feeling that my dad was seriously about to try to put me out, but it didn't matter because I already had a plan on wiping him out. Completely!

"All I'm saying is don't go flipping out on me. I didn't do anything!" I lied one more time before ending the call and preparing to pull up on him.

CHAPTER TWENTY-FOUR
TRICE

After applying my makeup and recurling my wig, I stopped to check my appearance in the mirror. I was trying my hardest to hide the way I was truly feeling. I was so broken that I felt like people could literally look at me and tell everything that I had been going through. My husband had left me. After years of me putting up with his cheating and lying, he fucking left me. I had gone to hell and back with his ass.

Choice had embarrassed me numerous times around the city. My biggest fear was always that he was going to leave me one day, but he always assured me and even his bitches that I was number one. He never went public with his shit, he made sure he came home to me, and he made sure he spoiled the hell out of me.

Ever since that Shawnie bitch got into the picture he had started acting differently. For starters, he was being stingy with his money. I mean, he still paid all the bills and shit, but now he was limiting what I could spend. And the only thing I could think of was there must be another woman. I knew about her way before I ever knew her name simply because of how he was acting. His actions and feelings never changed no matter how many women he cheated with, until now. Then when I would question him about anything he'd just find a way to reroute it to my drinking.

If I asked why he was being stingy with the money or limiting my spending, he'd say I'm not about to spend all his money on drinks. If I asked where he's been, he'd say don't nobody wanna be around that drunk shit all the time.

The issue with that was I had only been drinking heavier because I was trying to cope with him being gone. I had never had a drinking problem until about a year ago. I was going through the death of my parents and alcohol was my escape. Choice was mainly out in the streets fucking bitches and making money majority of the time. He'd come home and sleep with me but we weren't doing anything together anymore. No dates, no movie nights, baecations or anything. I was bored and miserable and before I knew it, I couldn't stop drinking.

Once I realized I had a problem, I immediately went to get help. I had been sober for about seven months before I accepted the fact that I wasn't strong enough to stop drinking. I decided to control my drinking by limiting myself. I hid it for a couple months but Choice eventually found out. And whenever he wanted to go do his bullshit, he would use that as an excuse.

Every time Choice would leave he would tear me down a little bit more. Calling me out my name, belittling me. It was like he hated me and was beginning to frown upon me. I knew he hated drunks because his mother was drunk the night she died. But he had no right to treat me like shit, especially when he drank, popped pills, and put cocaine up his nose. He did more than me. Yet he would always judge me and talk down on me about it.

He was trying to use my shortcomings and flaws to justify what he was doing with Shawnie. He had literally been gone for weeks. He hadn't gotten any clothes or anything. I wasn't stupid. I knew that meant he was filling her house up with clothes. Hell, maybe he had even bought her house.

My mind was racing about it. I was so depressed that I was physically losing weight. I felt like everyone in the world knew Shawnie, had seen her with my husband, and was now laughing at me. I was devastated, depressed, and feeling homicidal. I could kill that motherfucker for how he thought he was playing me. But I had a better plan.

I was going to ruin him. My husband thought he was doing something, but I was about to show the fuck out. I was going to take him for everything he had. In addition to that, I was going to expose him for the dirty, grimy motherfucker that he was. And I was going to start with his dad. I was going to expose all his lies! Not just the ones he was telling his dad but the ones he was telling his friends too.

Choice did so much devious shit to people. He played innocent all the time but normally was always the main person doing some bullshit to somebody. I had been watching him do snake shit to his father when his father and Shaniece were the only ones besides myself willing to do whatever for that man.

He was just a selfish, inconsiderate motherfucker. And if he thought I was going to throw away all these years I invested in him just to watch him run off into the sunset with another bitch, he had another thing coming.

"I got something for his ass!" I said after grabbing my car keys and rushing out to go find Wayne.

CHAPTER TWENTY-FIVE
WAYNE

"Is that going to be it for you?" the beautiful brown-skinned waitress at the diner by Wettler's asked me. I glanced at the menu one time before confirming my order with her.

"I'll be back in a few minutes with your food." She smiled politely before disappearing to the back. I sat there going through my notes on my phone, making sure there wasn't anything I was supposed to do that I had forgotten. After about a minute I heard a familiar voice call my name. I looked up to see my son's wife, Trice, standing in front of me. Her eyes were puffy and she looked like she was trying her hardest not to break down and cry.

"I ain't never seen you in here," Trice added, surprised. I could tell she was trying to make small talk to hide her true feelings.

"You know that I am a little everywhere," I replied.

"Do you mind if I sit here?" she asked. Without even giving me time to answer her question, she pulled out the chair and set down.

"What's going on, Trice?" I got straight to the point. I knew Trice had a way of always bringing drama in the mix and I didn't have time for it.

"Oh, don't act like you don't know," she hissed.

"Know about what?" I asked, completely clueless as to what she was talking about.

"My husband leaving me for your little worker!" she barked. I paused trying to think of what or who she could be referring to. I didn't even have any females on my roster. Not any that Choice would know anyways.

"Look, you got to stop bringing bullshit to us every time and you Choice get into it. We don't got shit to do with what y'all going through."

"Your son brings the bullshit and then y'all blame me for it. Like, it's okay for him to be fuckin' your workers but I can't pull up?"

"What worker are you talking about?"

"You know who I'm talking about. The one that helps Choice with the side business!" she barked.

"Choice not fucking any of my workers," I said seriously, but I couldn't help but wonder who she was talking about. I knew Trice had a reason to feel the way she was feeling. I was certain she wasn't just making it up. That was enough confirmation for me to know that my son really was out doing a bunch of bullshit under Wettler's, and I couldn't let that slide. I had to pick her for more information so I could have a better idea of what the fuck was going on.

"What makes you think whoever this girl is works for me?" I asked, damn near desperate to hear what she had to say. Something I said or the way I said it must've rubbed her the wrong way, because her entire demeanor changed. It was like she had realized I really didn't know what was going on, and now she wanted to protect Choice's secret.

"I'm so tired of everyone trying to play me like I'm crazy. I've dedicated my whole life to your son and he ain't done anything but dogged me out. He even cut my funds like I'm not the one taking care of his children," she whined before busting out into tears.

"What do you mean he cut your funds?" I asked, confused. One thing about my son was that he always took care of home. I simply couldn't believe that he would leave his wife and kids with no money. But he was so unpredictable that nothing really surprised me about him anymore.

"He's limiting what I can spend. After bills, I barely have enough money for food. But he's out here splurging on the next bitch!"

"How long has this been going on?"

"He's been gone for like two months. That's why I've been flipping out. I don't mean to bring drama to Wettler's. I love you and Shaniece. It's just when I get drunk I can't control myself. Wettler's is the only place I'm guaranteed to find him at." She took a break to try and regain her composure. She was breathing frantically like she was hyperventilating. Her face was becoming flushed and I was convinced she was about to crumble into pieces. I could see the pain consuming her and for the first time ever, I felt sorry for her.

"Don't cry, Trice," I said before getting up and wrapping my arms around her. My embrace seemed to bring the tears out more, but I didn't mind. I was a man and I knew the feeling of sadness. She needed to let that out and I was happy to be able to help her.

"I'm sorry you're going through this. But it isn't the end of the world. There's always something bigger and better out there," I explained to her while physically and emotionally wiping her tears.

"I'm going to give you some money to help with the kids. If

you need anything, feel free to reach out to me. I got you and the kids on whatever," I promised her before we both returned to our seats.

"Here you are, sir." The waitress returned with my food.

"Is there anything else I can get for you?" she asked, obviously inquiring about Trice. I looked at Trice waiting on her to respond, but she was so lost in my son's deception that she wasn't even paying attention.

"Trice?" I called her name to pull her out of the dark place her mind had placed her into.

"Yes?" she asked, still not aware of what was going on.

"Is there anything I can get you?" the woman asked again. I was grateful that she had good people skills and the patience to deal with Trice, because I knew one wrong move could send a scorned woman into rage.

"I'll have what he's having," Trice said dryly. I looked at her and smiled. She had always been so crazy that I'd never realized she had a soft side to her. A vulnerable side, and in the strangest way, she was starting to come off as sexy to me. I couldn't help but to think maybe she wasn't drama like everyone made her out to be. Maybe she was actually the victim, a good woman, and Choice was just fucking her up like he did everything and everyone else. Either way, I was going to give her the benefit of the doubt and make sure she and her kids were straight.

"Listen, I got some moves to make. I'm going to meet you at your house around four to drop you some money off," I said before dropping the money for our food on the table. She looked at me gratefully and smiled.

"Thanks for caring, Wayne," she said genuinely before standing up to hug me.

"No worries, doll. See you soon," I told her before going about my business.

CHAPTER TWENTY-SIX
SHANIECE

"Hey Auntie!" Vera sang happily as she walked into the gym. It was our thing to spend our mornings at the gym together from Tuesday till Saturday. It was something we had been doing for the last five years. We'd come together to vent, release our stress and worries through exercise, and wind down with lunch afterward.

"Hey baby, how are you?" I asked, knowing that her life was now becoming unpredictable as well thanks to Choice.

"I'm doing good!" she replied happily. Vera always managed to keep a positive outlook on life no matter what was going on. That was one of the main things I loved about her.

"And how is Chosen?" I asked with every intention to pry. I knew the heat from Choice's decision was burning Chosen in one way or another. And the more I knew about what was happening, the more I could figure out what Choice's ass was up too.

"Chosen is losing his mind, Auntie!" She sighed.

"What do you mean?" I asked, confused about what exactly he was doing.

"He's just been real overprotective since that little mall incident. He doesn't want me going anywhere now. And he bought me a gun."

"He's right too, because there is no telling who is on what. And nobody knows what's going on so everybody's moving off hearsay."

"They're saying that Choice has been burning bodies to help people get away with murder," she told me as if I wasn't aware of the rumors.

"I know what's being said. I've tried to talk to Wayne but I can't get him to listen to me. But now since he has that repast center up and running, Choice's ass doesn't have a reason to ever have his ass in Wettler's. I can't stand that little motherfucker and it pisses me the fuck off that Dwayne wanna play so dumb when it comes to his ass. That boy is bad news and he's been bad news. I want you to stay away from him," I told Vera seriously.

She smirked at me and shook her head as if she was implying I was crazy. I knew Vera the way a mother knew her own child. I knew she knew I wasn't crazy and she was always paying attention. Even when it didn't seem like it. I never had a problem venting to her or speaking my mind to her because I knew she valued my opinion and was always going to try and understand things from my point of view.

"What the hell?" I thought aloud after being distracted by a ding on my phone. Wayne had just withdrawn $5,000 out of one of our shared accounts and I wanted to know why.

"What's the matter?" Vera asked after hearing confusion in my tone.

"Nothing baby, Dwayne just always doing some bullshit!" I replied, not wanting to put Vera too much in our business. But it wasn't anything toward her, I was like that with everybody.

"I have to make a phone call," I told Vera before I took off toward the bathroom.

"Auntie, we be working out!" She she whined with her arms in the air.

"I'll be right back!" I promised her before dipping out. That workout would have to wait.

As soon as I got to the bathroom, I called Dwayne's phone. He didn't answer. That pissed me off so I called right back. He still didn't answer.

This motherfucker is doing some shit he don't got no business doing, I thought to myself. I could just feel it in my stomach. I knew my husband and I knew whatever he was doing had something to do with another woman. And I was for sure going to get to the bottom of it.

"Everything okay?" Vera asked once I got back. She had already jumped on the treadmill and started to break a sweat.

"Yea, I'm coo," I replied dryly before hopping on the treadmill next to her.

I didn't even waste any time jogging. I immediately started to run. I could feel Vera eyeballing me as if I had gone crazy. But I didn't care. I needed to work out harder so I could take my mind off all the crazy assumptions that were running through my mind.

Wayne had had affairs on me before. And I always found out because his behavior would start changing. He had sworn he would never cheat on me again and for some reason, I believed him. Or at least I wanted to. But the minute he moved wrong I was back at square one, not believing him again.

I had a certain insecurity when it came to Wayne. He was the finest of the finest and every girl wanted him. I never understood why he settled with me when I've seen him with so many other women. And I don't have low self-esteem or nothing like that, I'm just stating the obvious. I always had a feeling in the back of my mind that he was only around me for a come up. He didn't treat me like a come up or always have his hand out. It's just something I always felt. But I felt that about everybody. It just comes with being a millionaire I guess. Needless to say, if I was getting played like a fool, I wanted to know.

CHAPTER TWENTY-SEVEN
CHOICE

I sat outside the house I shared with Trice, debating on if I should even go inside. It had been about ten minutes and the thought alone of going inside was blowing me. I missed my kids like crazy, but I knew the moment I walked inside that house Trice was going to make me miserable. I had always been the type to stick it out for the kids, but after a couple months with Shawnie I didn't give a damn about sticking it out for them kids. As long as I provided for them and remained their father, I couldn't care less about them seeing me with another woman. I couldn't be miserable to please them or anybody else. Shawnie was who held my heart now and I wasn't about to do anything to fuck that up. After a few more minutes I decided to go inside and face the music.

Of course, the house was nasty as hell. There was a ton of TV dinner boxes piled up in the trash, so I knew my girls hadn't eaten a good meal for real. There were numerous tequila bottles laying around the house and it smelled like a pound of weed.

"Daddy!!" My youngest baby bear ran up to me and

jumped in my arms. I was so happy to feel her little touch that it saddened me that I couldn't give her a life with her mother and father in the same house forever. I was tempted to give in and try to make it work one last time before Trice came stumbling her drunk ass into the kitchen.

"That's crazy his ass can be gone for weeks with his other family and you all on his ass but want to walk around this motherfucker with an attitude at me," she snapped at my daughter, which immediately pissed me off.

"Nah, what's crazy is that you drunk at fucking ten in the morning yelling at my fucking daughter like she some bitch in the street." I immediately jumped to my baby's defense.

"Don't come in this motherfucker treating me like shit. You could've stayed where the fuck you were at," she slurred while almost falling over some trash that had piled up on the floor. I shook my head in disgust. I couldn't believe the person she had turned into. I honestly didn't even have any faith in her that she would ever do anything with her life. The way I saw it was she was only going down and incapable of moving up.

"Go upstairs, baby girl," I said to my daughter before kissing her on the forehead and placing her back on her feet. I knew I most likely was about to cuss Trice's ass out and maybe even slap her. I definitely didn't want my baby to witness that.

"Yea, go upstairs and pack a bag. Go with your dad!" Trice's drunk ass pitched in. That was it. I couldn't hold my cool anymore.

"Yea, go pack your bag and tell your sister to pack her bag too," I said in a way that let Trice know her drunk, petty bullshit wasn't stopping a motherfucking thing.

"So you think you finna have my kids around that bitch??" Trice immediately started tripping like she hadn't just suggested my kids go with me.

"They're going with me. It shouldn't matter who the fuck

they're around. That's your problem, you're always worried about the wrong shit!"

"Me confronting you about you cheating on me is being worried about the wrong shit?"

"I'm not cheating on you! We're not together and haven't been together for months. Fuck is wrong with you?"

"How can you say that and I'm your wife?" she asked, seemingly heartbroken. It drove me crazy how she always played so innocent like she was a victim. I had been cheating on her since the very beginning. She knew what she was signing up for. But no matter what I always made sure home was good. So once she intentionally did something to fuck up what I'm trying to do, I'on be trying to fuck with her no more. She knew that.

"You just out here dogging me. Embarrassing the fuck out of me. For a bitch you don't even know," she added before I could even answer her last question.

"Okay, well leave me alone. Divorce me and get the fuck on," I finally said the very thing I had been wanting to say to her. I could tell it broke her and a small part of me broke too, but oh well. I couldn't keep going through that shit. I could be happy and co-parent without fucking with her.

"You want a divorce? Bitch, is you serious?" she growled at me. I knew right away she was about to try and fight me. "After everything I've been through with you? You think you're just about to throw me out like a piece of trash?" she hissed.

I watched her heartbreak turn into rage right before my eyes. I got a real bad feeling that something was about to happen. I wanted so badly to end things between us peacefully, but the fact that she was so drunk was making me want to say fuck everything.

"Listen, you carrying yourself like trash. This shit is not

working. I been warning you for months," I tried to explain myself, but that clearly was a bad idea.

"Warning me?!?" she screamed in a way that let me know it was about to go the fuck down. Before I could say or do anything, she had grabbed her gun out of her purse and aimed it at me. I had already taken off when I saw her grab for it, but she still shot at me as I ran to my car. I had no choice but to pull off, leaving my kids with the fuckin' devil herself.

CHAPTER TWENTY-EIGHT

TRICE

I was so pissed off at Choice that I was literally shaking. I couldn't believe that motherfucker had the audacity to walk into our home talking bout 'bout he wants a fucking divorce. After everything I did for him. After everything I put up with. All the lies, all the cheating, him becoming abusive when he was high, all type of shit that the next woman wouldn't even stick around for. Yet he thought he was just going to up and leave me?

Choice had me fucked up, and now I was really going to set his ass up for failure. He had to be crazy as hell to really believe he would be able to get that shit off with me. Like if you're going to cheat, cheat! Don't come in this bitch asking for no fucking divorce though. He had some fucking nerve.

I hurried to my kitchen to grab a bottle of tequila from my bar. Most people would say that drinking was never the answer, but it was for me. I needed a shot more than anything at that moment. I poured one shot and tossed it back as quickly as possible. Then another. Before I could get to my third shot, someone was knocking on the door.

"Who the fuck is it?" I yelled before grabbing my gun and heading to the door. I was surprised to see Wayne standing there with his gun out. He looked at me like he was surprised to see me alive.

"You came here to shoot me?" I asked straight out.

"What? No. There's casings all over your porch and a bullet through your screen door. I just was preparing for whatever was next," he said honestly. He placed his gun on his hip and came closer to me. "Give me the gun," he said calmly. I took a second to think about it but before I could make up my mind, he was taking the gun out of my hand.

"Tell me what's going on," he demanded genuinely. He wrapped his arms around me and I allowed myself to melt in his embrace. I had never in a million years imagined I'd be seeking comfort from Wayne but man, I was loving that shit. He was nothing like his son. So much stronger and manlier and just overall better. He was attentive, gentle, and protective all in the same sense.

"Did the girls see this?" he asked after hearing another lie I had told him. I made him think that his son came to my house tweaking out on drugs and I was forced to shoot back at him after he tried to kill me.

"No, I had already sent them upstairs."

"And what is he upset about?"

"He's upset because I spent $500 off his card. But I had no choice. He literally limited my spending. Our lights were about to be cut off." I started to cry and Wayne held me tighter. It was like the softest place on earth. As crazy as it may sound, it was the only place I wanted to be.

"Don't cry," Wayne told me as he continuously caressed my top and lower back. I could tell he wanted to do way more for me but he was holding back. I assumed it was out of respect for his son but I didn't give a damn bout 'bout respecting Choice. I wanted to do what would make me happy. Sleeping around with Wayne seemed like the answer to my problems. And after seeing how easily persuaded he was by a few tears, I knew eventually I was going to get him.

"Look, I brought you some money," Wayne said apologetically. I could tell he knew money wouldn't fix everything and was willing to go that extra mile to fix the rest. "Is there anything else I can do for you?" he asked after handing me five thousand dollars. He was so bossy that it made my pussy throb. I couldn't understand how such a boss ass nigga could birth such a disloyal, greedy little bitch like Choice.

"Stay the night with me?" I asked the question that had been running through my mind since he entered my presence. He paused for a minute and looked at me confused. I could tell he didn't trust me and maybe even felt like it was a set up a little bit. I started to regret asking him a question like that so fast. I was convinced he was about to say no and was desperate to clean it up while I still had time.

"I don't mean it like that." I tried to hurry up and undo any damage, but from the looks of it there wasn't much damage done.

"It's cool. I'll stay," he said, cutting my attempts of rewording my request short. He gave me another hug and smiled.

"You're going to be fine. I got you. I promise," he added before kissing me on my forehead. His touch and embrace literally made me feel like all my problems were going away. And even though my original plan was to use Wayne to get back at Choice, I wanted something completely different now with Wayne. And I was going to get it.

CHAPTER TWENTY-NINE
VERA

I stared at Chosen as we rode in silence. He was so upset. I hated seeing him that way, but man was he fine as hell. He had this little habit of clenching his jaw bone when he was mad and it just sent me through ecstasy every time I saw him do it. In addition to that, all of his veins popped out whenever he was mad. I don't know why, but it turned me on so bad. The veins in his hands, his forehead, pretty much everywhere. It was hard for him to hide when he was upset. Especially from someone like me, who noticed every little detail about him.

"Are you going to tell me what's got you so upset?" I asked after a few more minutes of silence. He looked at me and smiled softly before patting me on my thigh. As crazy as it may sound, I knew that was his way of telling me to shut the hell up. I wasn't about to pry. I was just going to wait until he was ready to talk about it. But I damn sure wasn't about to listen to no damn drill music.

I knew how important energy was and how it could be transformed by music and other things. I would be a fool if I let my man ride around listening to drill while he was mad. The whole damn city would be dropping dead and my man would be in jail. I wasted no time turning the song.

"Vera!" he said my name in a obviously irritated tone once I turned from King Von to Lauryn Hill. I tried my hardest not to bust out laughing.

"What? I don't want to hear that drill shit. I'm not the homie and we ain't finna go slide!" I replied sarcastically. He looked at me and smiled. I was happy to at least see a smile on his face.

"Shut up, girl! You is my homie," he responded in a joking manner. Clearly my decision to play Lauryn Hill was the right move, because he hadn't said so much as two words to me since we got in the car.

"So what's this meeting about?" I asked since my man didn't seem as angry anymore. He and my aunt had already told me that we all were expected to attend a meeting.

"I'm pretty sure it has something to do with Choice," Chosen replied irritably. I couldn't help but to understand his frustration. He literally was fighting bodies behind his brother's mistakes. He had to look over his shoulder now and he was trying to force me to live that way too. Choice hadn't even so much as said sorry about the shit. All he did was keep acting like he had no reason as to why everyone was so upset.

"I'm sick of that motherfucker, man." My man was finally venting to me. I wasn't going to interrupt him either. I was just going to let him get his funky off. It was better than him going out and fucking up his brother. Or even worse, shooting somebody else.

"For real, his ass putting everybody ass on the line for some shit none of us got anything to do with," he continued to vent as we arrived at Wettler's.

I was shocked to see so many cars there. I knew that my

aunt Shaniece and uncle Wayne didn't have that many employees. There had to be something else going on.

"You sure this is just a meeting we're going to?" I asked, referring to the massive amount of cars there.

"I'm going to the meeting. You're going to the ribbon cutting ceremony at the repast center."

"We're is my aunt at?" I asked confused about why somebody always felt the need to make decisions for me.

"Can you just do what I said, please?" Chosen low key snapped at me. I knew he wasn't trying to be mean to me but I got tired of him treating me like I was a fuckin' kid. I couldn't stand it.

"I'm just going to stay in the car!" I replied rudely. I didn't like no last-minute changes and nobody had said anything about us having to split up. I wanted to know what the hell was going on just like everybody else.

"Vera, get yo' ass out of this car and go support your aunt in her new accomplishments," he hissed at me like he was about to spank me.

"Go 'head on to your meeting that's so fuckin' confidential." I was just about to start talking shit before he placed his hands around my neck.

"Stop doing that, please," he said in the softest, sweetest tone while kissing my earlobes. "I'on want to be in here no more than you do. Let's just do what we gotta do and be out of here, please!" he told me before passionately sticking his tongue into my mouth. "Do what I said, please," he demanded in a way that made my kitty purr.

"Okay! I'll see you in a minute." Without another word, I fully submitted to his will. I knew he had my best interest at heart and no matter what, I knew he would be back. I knew he was already stressed out, fighting bodies, living with murder on his conscious, looking over his shoulder, and looking his brother in the eye every day without fucking him up. Even though he wanted to so badly.

I let him handle the situation his way because one thing for certain was, I didn't want my man mad at me for not listening to him. Then with all the shit going down with Choice, I ain't want to be at no motherfucking meeting with his ass no way. The damn feds might be in that motherfucker and then we'd all go down just for knowing that motherfucker. Hell no, I was good. I happily walked over to the ribbon cutting and joined the crowd.

CHAPTER THIRTY
SHAWNIE

The sound of my phone ringing jerked me from the deep sleep I had fallen into. I knew for sure whoever was calling was serious about getting in touch with me because I had heard the phone ring multiple times while I was asleep. I jumped up and grabbed the phone, curious to know who the hell was blowing my phone up and what they wanted.

"Shit!" It was my child's father, Scar, calling me. I hurried to try and answer it but I wasn't fast enough. I redialed the number but not before I noticed that I also had missed calls from Detective Randolph. I was just about to decide who to call back before Scar called me back. It wasn't until then that I realized Choice's ass wasn't even in the bed with me. I hurried up and ran to my bathroom to answer the call.

"Hello?" I tried to sound as normal as possible once I answered. I turned on the shower to drown out the sound since I had no clue where Choice was. As far as I knew he could've been on the other side of the door listening to my conversation, and I definitely couldn't afford that.

"What the fuck is you doing to where you can't answer the phone?" Scar barked at me. It broke my heart immediately because I knew that meant he was worried or stressed. Scar wasn't naturally violent with me and whenever he was raising his voice there was a hidden reason I'd always find. He never just talked crazy to me. But he did stay on my ass. He most definitely was what one would call a fan of tough love.

"I'm so sorry. I've been busy," I explained to him. My life had gotten so chaotic that I wasn't even an early bird how he was used to me being anymore.

"Okay, so tell me something," Scar added, insinuating that I give him an update about our son.

"I haven't found him yet. But I have a good idea of what happened. I'm real close though," I explained to him in a way that let him know what was going on but also kept Choice in the dark if he was eavesdropping.

"Have you thought about asking your boyfriend? Because word on the streets is that your boy Choice accepted an offer from his friends Marty and Quan to dispose of Trell's body through his family funeral home after a robbery gone wrong. They also saying Trell took one of them out with him," my babydad filled me in on a story that was so similar to what I had already put together.

"Wait, how do you know that is true?" I asked, confused about who his source was.

"Man, do I look like the type of nigga you need to question?" he said seriously to me.

"You know what, you're right! I apologize."

"Yea girl, because you know I'm not finna steer you in the wrong direction."

"I know baby, there are just so many different stories going around," I tried to explain my reasoning for questioning him.

"You wanna hear another story going around?"

"What's that, Scar?"

"I'll be home in six months. I got a sentence reduction. I'm coming straight to you," he said proudly. My entire body lit up as I slowly started to overflow with joy. Now Scar was someone I loved. I was crazy in love with him. Losing our son had been so tough that nobody else had been able to comfort me properly and help me grieve. It was like nobody understood me but him. I needed him more than anybody else.

"Are you fucking kidding me right now?" I asked in shock.

"Nope. I'll be there, baby. Be ready for me," he said before ending the call. I was salty he didn't say goodbye, but I understood. There probably was a guard or something that was coming and he didn't want to lose his cell phone. Nevertheless, I didn't call back. I just was grateful for the time we did get to talk.

Before I could even put my phone down and put some soap on me, my phone was ringing again. It was Detective Randolph. I hurried to answer the call, letting him know right off top to make it snappy.

"Yes, speak to me!"

"We have the warrant. We will be going into Wettler's within the next hour," he announced happily.

"I'm pretty sure everything is out of the way now," I said irritably. They knew after that meeting that catching Wayne in a mess wasn't going to be easy. The whole entire point of him having the meeting was to acknowledge to everyone face to face that he had no knowledge of what his son was doing and begging them not to offer any more jobs. He did the shit so smooth to where I'm a whole agent and there was nothing I could do but blow my cover if I were to try to respond.

Me and my other partner, Raj, could tell right away that Wayne and Shaniece had the time to put their ducks in a row and get their building together. Honestly, I felt like Raj and

Randolph were wasting their time. But I guess it was still worth the shot.

"You and Raj stay back until you hear from me. We need you guys' cover safe. No matter what, do not get involved in this," Randolph advised me before hanging up the phone. I rolled my eyes, irritated by his demanding commands. I then grabbed the towel and patted myself dry.

Suddenly, I got this feeling that something was extremely wrong. But I couldn't for the life of me figure out what it was. I continued to pat myself dry as I exited the bathroom door.

"Choice? What are you doing?" I asked, a little startled by the fact that he had been sitting right on the other side of that door.

"I'm cool on you. I ain't tryna fuck with you no more," Choice said dryly before leaving out of the house. I was so caught off guard that I couldn't even call out for him to wait. I didn't even know what he was upset about. All I knew was that I had more than one secret he would be mad about. The issue was which one had he found out.

CHAPTER THIRTY-ONE
SHANIECE

"What the fuck is your problem, Shaniece?" Dwayne screamed at me as I continued to walk around Wettler's ignoring him. It just wasn't enough that his son had my company name in all types of bullshit. He had to go ahead and add to the mix. Wayne was already doing a separate side hustle in which he was moving drugs through champagne bottles at the repast center.

"You're just selfish as fuck!" I yelled at him. And it was the truth. He wondered why his son was the way he was, but I always said it was because of him. Choice wasn't doing anything but following in his father's footsteps. The only difference was that Choice was messy with his shit.

"How the fuck am I selfish? I bought that repast center to keep our family employed and keep your father's company protected from any bullshit my kids got into."

"Speaking of bullshit, you wanna tell me what you took five thousand dollars out of our account for?" I decided to ask the question I had already been sitting on.

"Five thousand dollars?" He looked confused for a second as he tried to comprehend what I was talking about.

"Yes, five thousand dollars. Last week." I spoke clearly so that I could refresh his memory.

"I didn't know it came out of our joint account. My apologies. I gave that to Trice to help get her and the kids away from some bullshit Choice got them into."

"Trice?" I couldn't believe what I was hearing. My husband barely even talked to that girl and now he was dropping five racks on her. Hell no. I was far from dumb and one thing I knew about my husband was when he was hiding something. Something was going on between him and Trice or he would have just told me about the situation. I would've never had to question him in the first damn place. That's for damn sure.

"Since when did you start dealing with that bitch?" I decided to dig deeper, just to see what all I could find. My husband's demeanor seem agitated but I didn't give a damn. I wasn't about to get played like boo-boo the fool, especially by a motherfucker whose son was trying to sink my company.

"I wasn't dealing with her. I ran into her at the diner and she told me Choice had left and limited her money for the girls. She was behind on bills and all. So I gave her that money to stay afloat. She is my grandkids' mother you know," he said matter-of-factly. It burnt me up that he was talking to me like I didn't have a reason to be suspicious.

"What the hell am I supposed to think, Dwayne?" I yelled with tears pooling in my eyes. "It's not like you've never cheated!" I whined, and before a tear could even fall from my eyes, my husband had wrapped his arms around me.

"I know it's getting tough but we already made it through the hard part," he said, kissing me on my forehead. "I need us to please stick together right now so we can come out on top later," he explained to me before lifting my face up and kissing me on the lips. I decided to relax under his advice instead of continuously working myself up over things I couldn't control.

"We already got a lot of people working against us," he told me as he waited on me to calm down. I wasted no time getting back to my normal self. If my husband wasn't right about anything else, he was right about us needing to stick together.

"You're right, baby!" I verbally admitted to him. That was my way of surrendering to his will and letting him know I was giving him full control over the situation. He was my man and I trusted him to lead just as well as I trusted myself to lead.

"Mrs. Wettler?" I heard a very familiar and unfriendly voice call out my name. I turned to see Detective Randolph standing in my waiting area.

"What the hell do y'all pig ass motherfuckers want now?" I immediately started to talk shit to him.

"What do you mean? I told you I would be back with a warrant!" he boasted. I looked at my husband, confused and wondering if he still wanted me to 'trust him.' He glanced back at me and telepathically gave me permission to speak.

"A warrant for what?" I asked, confused.

"A warrant to search the property. Now don't play dumb," Detective Randolph said snottily.

"That's right. We have a warrant to search every inch of this place." Before I could even respond, Chief Connor was in there bumping his fat ass gums and waving around his warrant.

"This is ridiculous. How do you get a warrant off hearsay? Nobody's selling no damn drugs," I said proudly, knowing that I had cleaned every nook and cranny in that place.

"Oh, we're not here for drugs. We're here looking for evidence in connection to the disappearance of Latrell Warner," Detective Randolph proudly added.

I looked at them, confused about what or who they were

talking about. I tried my hardest not to scream at the top of my lungs or attack my husband as I processed what was going on.

"Wait a minute, who the fuck is Latrell?" Dwayne asked the same question I was thinking.

"Probably somebody they made up!" I replied sarcastically. I had to stand my ground in some kind of way. I couldn't let them see me sweat.

"Oh yeah?" Detective Randolph asked as he posted up a picture of Latrell Warner. My heart dropped down to the bottom of my ass. I knew that little boy. It was the same unidentified body I had seen on that table. I never forgot his face simply because I thought he had been left unidentified as a mistake on my staff's behalf. I had no idea he was a missing person. Somebody's baby. My heart broke immediately and no matter how hard I tried to hide it, I knew everyone in the room saw that.

"Anything you wanna tell us?" Detective Randolph asked sarcastically.

"Yea, do what y'all got to do and get the fuck out my shit!" I barked back, hoping and praying they didn't find anything to connect us to Latrell. I was more than positive we were good on the drugs side, but the DNA side was a little different. I couldn't help but to worry.

"Who was it?" my husband asked, referring to the picture the cops had shown me.

"This is all you and your fucking son's fault," I hissed at him. I knew he didn't have anything to do with it, but he was the only one who could've stopped it and he didn't.

"I don't even know what the fuck is going on," he replied, confused about my energy toward him. His phone started to ring and this motherfucker looked at it and stepped off. I immediately got offended because who the hell was so important that you have to walk off from a conversation as serious as the one we were having?

"I'll be there in a second," I heard him say before stepping back up to me.

"I got to go. Something is going down. Call me when this is finished," he said before sprinting off to his car.

CHAPTER THIRTY-TWO

TRICE

After finding and stealing $150,000 from my husband, I trashed the house to stage a robbery. I then woke my kids up in a panic and made them run through the woods to get to our neighbor's house.

"Go call your papa G and tell him someone broke into the house and Mommy is in danger," I informed my oldest daughter. I knew I could trust her to get the job done.

I spent about five more minutes cleaning out any small valuables I could collect. Jewelry, guns, money! Anything I could get my hands on. I was going to leave Choice high and dry. And I was going to have his father protect me while I did it.

"What happened?" Wayne jumped out of the car and hugged me and the kids. The way he jumped out surprised me. Because it was as if he actually cared. Hell, I was shocked to see how fast he had made it to us.

"Please, get me out of here!" I pretended to be in fear for my life, playing my role to a tee. He wasted no time putting us in the car and getting us away from the danger I had made up.

"I got to holla at your momma. Make yourself at home,

y'all go in there and get a snack or something," Wayne told my kids after we arrived to a luxurious condo downtown. The girls clearly felt safe and had no problem listening to him. The moment they dipped into the kitchen, he grabbed me by my hand and pulled me to one of the back rooms.

I had to admit it, the condo was nice. And because he took me there thinking I was in danger, I assumed it was a duck-off spot that nobody else knew about. I knew for sure Choice wasn't going to know about it because he did too damn much. Wayne never told him anything, and the little bit of shit he did know about, he was fucking it up already.

"Have you spoken with Choice?" he asked once we were alone. I shook my head no, still staring at his lips as he spoke. It made my panties wet just watching his tongue slide across his lips when he ended a sentence. And he wasn't even trying to be flirtatious. His aura was just sexy.

"Are you going to tell me what's going on or what?" he asked after not getting an answer from me the first time. This time he pushed me up against the wall and pressed his body against mine.

"You can trust me, Trice. I'm not going to let anything happen to your or them babies. Please tell me what's going on so I can fix it." He was begging me. I could feel his heart beating against my chest. I held my breath and imagined kissing him. He smelled so good, like cologne, za, and backwood cigars. I hated the smell of marijuana on Choice but it smelt so good on his daddy. It was intoxicatingly enticing. Everything about him was enticing to me. I wanted to stay in that moment forever, yet I couldn't help but feel like I needed to walk away from him. I was playing a dangerous game and even though Wayne was falling into my little plan, I was still taking one hell of a risk even trying it. He grabbed my face and gently directed my gaze to his.

"What's got you so scared, Trice? Did my son hit you?" he asked again. This time there was something different in his tone, but I couldn't figure out what it was. I looked at him with eyes pleading for him to just drop it, but I could tell he wasn't going to. But it was fine because I had had more than enough time to get my story straight.

"Someone tried to kill us. I don't know who it was. I saw them pulling up on the camera while me and the kids were in the back. My first instinct was to run into the woods with the kids and run toward the neighbors," I told him a lie that was fitting to the cause.

"Did you get a look at their faces?"

"Yes, but only one of them. There were at least three people."

"What else did you see?" he asked as if he was a detective investigating the case.

"That's it really, I just took off running. I had to get my kids out of there." I pretended to cry my heart out. I purposely fell into his arms, desperate to feel him close to me again.

"Do you think Choice would try to kill me?" I asked, confused.

"Not Choice, but prolly someone he pissed off. Don't even trip though. I'ma take care of it," he added in a way that made me want to pounce on his dick right then and there. It was so hard for me to hold my composure. I was so into that man that I was losing sight of the real plan, which was getting back at Choice's bitch ass.

CHAPTER THIRTY-THREE
WAYNE

"Can you relax and let me handle this?" I placed my hand on the wall right next to Trice's head and leaned toward her. The thought of kissing her crossed my mind. I wanted to kiss her. But I didn't. I knew it would be wrong, but I was honestly forming a weak spot for her. Fighting my feelings for her was starting to become like fighting a street war. It wasn't anything to play with. Still, I was going to keep her close to me.

"Y'all can stay here till I get everything figured out. You don't have to worry 'bout food or anything. I'ma take care of y'all," I promised.

She stared at me confused. After reading her I got the feeling that she didn't know whether she should trust me or fear me. For all she knew, me being so helpful could've been a setup. And I couldn't blame her for being cautious. Especially after dealing with my son.

"Wayne, why are you doing this?" She decided to ask the question that I already knew she was thinking. The crazy part about that was I didn't have the answer for her. I was low key intimidated by her bluntness and at a loss for words.

"Doing what?" I asked, completely lost.

"Doing this!?!" She pointed at the small space between us. "Why are you doing this? What the fuck do you want from me?" she snapped.

The hurt in her voice broke my heart for some reason and I wanted nothing more than to comfort her and show her genuine love. She was becoming my weakness and I couldn't understand how. No matter how bad I wanted her, I knew I had to shake her off. I couldn't afford to be vulnerable for her, not with all the crazy shit I already had going on.

"Is it sex? Is that what you want?" She throw a curve ball in the mix. She wanted to pick my brain and see where she stood with me. That was more than obvious.

"You think I'm doing this shit for some pussy, Trice?" The tone in my voice made her feel silly for asking. But I could tell she didn't care. I could tell from the way she looked at me she wanted me. The way she talked and the fact that anytime she needed me she would call and I'd come running. So she knew the feeling was mutual.

And I was positive she was keeping it between us too, because my wife or my son would have been spoke on it.

Truth is that I wanted nothing more than to feel inside of her. I lowered my head, not even wanting to face her. I was afraid she could see through me. I felt like she could read my thoughts.

"Let me show you something," I said confidently.

I wrapped my arms around her waist and turned her around so that she was facing me. Then I placed her on the bed. I watched as she sat there with lust in her eyes. I could see it going deeper. She had lust in her heart as she watched me take my shirt off. I knew exactly what she was thinking because I'd seen that look on other women. Their response was always the same.

"Oh Wayne, you don't look your age at all!" Or "you look better than your son." It was funny to me because they assumed because my kids were grown I was old. But really I just started young. Still, my body was solid as hell. And I could melt any woman.

I placed my hand on her shoulder and gently pushed her back on the bed before climbing on top of her. I paid close attention as her body started to scream for joy.

For a minute, I thought she was going to resist me. But once small moans started escaping her throat I knew I could have her. And I was going to have her. She opened her legs and pulled me closer to her. I knew that was her way of giving me the invitation I already had.

I began to grind between her legs. Just enough to show her how I could master her. Then she kissed me. Our very first kiss. Though she wasn't speaking any words, her kiss said so much. I had never felt so much emotion in a kiss. Especially a kiss with a person I had no business kissing. Somehow, it felt like I had known her my entire life. And it wasn't through my son.

I paused briefly, long enough for us to stare into each other's eyes. I shot my gaze down to her stomach and then back up to her eyes. She followed my eyes every step of the way. I had her full attention. And I couldn't help but to admire the moment. She was beautiful. Rare and special. And I was starting to realize I wasn't going to be able to get enough of her.

"What's wrong, Wayne? What are you thinking about?" she asked, hoping to get a glimpse of what my thoughts were. I answered her with another kiss. She moaned into my mouth as I pushed my hands down her body and in between her legs. I just had to touch her and feel what she felt like.

She started to shake at the touch of my hands against her throbbing pussy. It was like her panties were melting. It felt like there was nothing in between us but both our desires to fuck.

"Do you want me to stop?" I whispered into her ear. She immediately shook her head no and reached up for another kiss. I met her halfway. We kissed for what seemed like eternity and then I stopped again.

"I'm going to get y'all set up here until I can figure out what's going on." I had to kiss her one more time, then I quickly hopped up and started putting my shirt back on. I was going to come back for her in due time. For now, I had to make sure she knew I was just after sex. But at least now she knew I could get it if I wanted it.

She laid there dumbfounded with her legs still open, shaking, and waiting on me to enter her. She knew I wanted her and I could tell she couldn't understand why I did what I did. And that was okay because one day it was all going to make sense.

CHAPTER THIRTY-FOUR
CHOICE

I came back out from the gas station to see that I already had six missed calls. "What the fuck?" I asked, confused as ever. I had only been away from my phone for about five minutes. There was no way I should've been getting blown up like that. Unless something was wrong. Upon further inspection, I realized that the majority of the calls were from Shaniece. The other two were from Shawnie.

I immediately frowned when I saw her ass calling me. I wasn't feeling her at all. The one thing I disliked the most and couldn't accept from someone was disloyalty. And Shawnie was disloyal for no reason. She just didn't think I knew.

See, Shawnie had this thing where she would have to go to the bathroom to answer her phone whenever I was around. Naturally, that made me decide to install surveillance throughout the crib I had got for us. I had been so busy trying to get my bag up so I could make things move for me and her that I hadn't really gotten the chance to watch the videos until the other day. There were about five days in a row where she answered a call at the same time every day. Whoever was calling was someone she had to answer to because she was always reporting back to them. What confused me the most was the fact that she was always talking in codes like she was a cop or something.

Either way, after watching days of that footage, I realized there was a lot about Shawnie that I didn't really know. I never had to wonder what Trice was doing behind my back because I knew where her loyalty lied at. I didn't even need cameras around the house with Trice, but when I did test her she passed with flying colors each time.

That damn Shawnie was something different. I was starting to get a bad feeling about her and I usually wasn't ever wrong about those feelings. The way she spoke on that phone was so weird. I could never hear the other caller but I could tell that they were speaking in codes, and there wasn't ever anyone possibly listening but me. So what was she hiding and who was she talking to every morning?

She couldn't be trusted and I definitely wasn't willing to give up my life with Trice for a disloyal bitch. I didn't care how good she made me feel. That shit don't mean anything if it isn't real.

I wanted so badly to call Trice but I couldn't bring myself to do it. I had asked her for a divorce and I knew that broke her. And for what? All for a bitch I couldn't even trust. I bet Trice's ass would love to rub that shit in my face too. I wasn't even about to give her the satisfaction of being able to do that. I decided to hold off calling her. Simply because I knew as long as I could convince her it had nothing to do with Shawnie, she would work extra hard to fix the things about herself that I didn't like. Versus having something else to throw up in my face whenever she got upset. I decided to play by my own rules once again.

The sound of my phone ringing pulled me from my thoughts and back to reality. It was Shaniece again.

"What the fuck does she want?" I asked, confused as to why she felt the need to blow my phone up. Not sure if something was wrong, I decided to answer this time.

"Wassup Shaniece?" I answered.

"Don't you wassup me. We're not cool and if you think I'm going to let my family's company burn in a fire you started, you have another thing coming," she hissed the moment she heard my voice. I paused, confused about what the hell she was even talking about.

"What are you talking about now, Shaniece?" I asked, irritated with her complaining as usual.

"The police just left from here looking for evidence about some missing person."

"What that got to do with me?"

"I saw him myself! I'm not going down for your shit. For your sake, you just better hope nothing comes back. Because I'm letting you know now, I'm not going down for your shit."

"So what, you saying you're going to rat me out to the pigs?" I asked, wanting to be sure I understood what she was getting at.

"What I'm saying is, I ain't going down for your shit. I want you to stay far the hell away from my business. You fuckin' monster," she yelled before hanging up the phone on me. I had never heard her so angry, and I was certain whatever happened was serious to make her panic like that.

I decided to swallow my pride and head on home. I had about 200K in cash put up there for me and my family to run off with. I couldn't think of a better time to do that than now. Especially with all the weird shit going on around me. I couldn't help but feel like I was about to go to jail or get killed.

The feeling was getting stronger and stronger. I had to get away.

I called Trice's phone but she didn't answer. She hadn't answered for a couple days so I figured I would just drive there to see her. I stopped at the store and brought her some flowers just to make my return a little more desirable for her. But truth was, I knew she was mad at me. And for real, she prolly was done with me.

"Trice?" I called out to her once I entered the house. A very strange feeling came over me as I looked around the house. It looked ransacked but with no sign of forced entry. All my wife and kids' clothes and things were spread all throughout the house and there wasn't a sign of any of them around.

I pulled out my gun and immediately searched the rest of the house for them. I couldn't find them. I then ran to my man cave to look for the 200K that I was supposed to deliver for Raj. The job wasn't due till next week but I was definitely about to use it for a rainy day. I didn't give a damn about Raj and I didn't fear him. I was more than willing to go to war with him behind that money. Only thing was, it was gone. Every dollar of it was gone.

"That fucking bitch!" I snapped, realizing that my wife had robbed me and put me into deeper shit than what I already was in.

CHAPTER THIRTY-FIVE
SHAWNIE

My heart was nearly beating out of my chest as I waited inside the donut shop for Detective Randolph and Raj to join me for breakfast. As hungry as I was, I couldn't eat a thing because I was so nervous to hear what Randolph had to tell me. I just knew it wasn't anything good. I could feel the shit in my stomach.

What's even crazier was I could feel my son was dead the night he died. That very next morning I went out searching for him. We found a massive amount of his blood that suggested he had some type of fatal injury. The problem was we couldn't find his body anywhere. So my son never got a proper burial or anything. He just was gone without a trace.

Once I heard about what was happening at Wettler's, I immediately knew that's what had to have happened to my son as well. There was no other explanation and it angered me that authorities ain't do shit about it for real. They could've been run in that place over one of the other claims before my son and maybe my son would still be here. Or we would at least be able to investigate and get justice for him. I just couldn't understand how Choice or anybody else could completely disregard someone's life or death for a dollar.

My original reason for getting close with Choice was to get to the bottom of what happened to my son. But now, after seeing how much of a heartless and cold-hearted monster he was, I had a change of plans. I wanted him dead. I wanted to make sure no other mother had to cry my tears and no other woman had to cry his wife's tears either.

Choice was just a dog all around the board. I watched him get a whiff of this pussy and say fuck his entire family. A woman who dedicated her entire life to him and he kicked her to the curb for a piece of random pussy. He didn't know me from Adam and Eve and he clearly didn't value the woman he did know. My son would never treat anyone he cared for with such indecency. My son did not ever deserve to cross paths with that motherfucker. I don't give a fuck if he was already dead. Choice was an animal and I was going to make sure he got handled. And it was either going to be by myself or by my son's dad.

"Hey baby cakes," Randolph said to me as he and Raj took a seat opposite of me. I could tell from the tone in his voice that he had bad news for me.

"Just give it to me straight," I said to him. I knew he most likely was hesitant about whatever it was he wanted to tell me.

"He was there, wasn't he?" I asked straight out. Raj put his head down while Detective Randolph sighed with disappointment.

"The evidence is kind of sketchy because it's been damaged and mixed with so many other DNAs. I did, however, locate this," Detective Randolph said before pulling out a small evidence baggie. I hurriedly grabbed the baggie and almost fainted when I realized it contained my son's car key fob. He was a Steelers fan and his fob was customized specifically to his liking. I could never forget it.

"They burned my baby!" I began to cry the cry I had been holding on to for months. I knew he was gone but a part of me was still hoping for a proper burial. But I knew now that that wasn't possible.

"So what's next? Are you about to make an arrest?" I asked, curious to hear what the plan was.

"See, that's the thing. We didn't actually have a warrant to search it. We had to do what we had to do because we were running out of time."

"So we can't use any of this in court?" I asked, confused.

"Listen, at least this way you have some answers and we can still use Raj to take those motherfuckers down." Randolph tried to speak positively but I wasn't trying to hear that shit.

I was going to get revenge for my son starting with Choice and then going after everybody around him.

"I have persuaded Choice to agree to one more drop. It's 200K in marked cash from a guest in Texas. If he gets caught doing it, he will do life in prison guaranteed," Raj explained.

"It'll be easy peezy getting a confession about his part in Latrell's murder after that. We also have a new approach to hit Shaniece with too," Randolph said.

"What do you mean?" I asked, confused about Shaniece's role in all this.

"Her husband is having an affair with Choice's wife," Raj said happily as he slid over some pictures of Wayne and Trice going at each other. The two were kissing uncontrollably and unable to keep their hands off each other. It shocked the hell out of me but also made me smile. That's what Choice's ass got. I knew this news would devastate him. It would devastate

Shaniece even worse. This was the type of ammo that could ruin their entire organization.

"Now this is more like it!" I said with satisfaction oozing out of my tone. I knew for sure we were finally about to get somewhere.

CHAPTER THIRTY-SIX
CHOSEN

"Wake up, love," I whispered as I gently kissed Vera out of her sleep. She looked so beautiful to me. She was literally perfect and I could not be happier to have her all to myself. In the center of all the madness, Vera was my peace and I needed her to know how much that meant to me. I wanted to go out of my way to let her know how special she was to me and today was going to be the day.

"What time is it?" she asked before she even had her eyes opened. I knew she wasn't too happy about being woken up at 5 a.m., but once she saw what I had planned for her she was going to forget all about what time she had to wake up.

"Get up baby, we got somewhere to be," I told her. She opened her eyes fully and looked at me confused.

"Chosen, what are you talking about?" she asked, obviously not down for playing the guessing game.

"Just come on. I got your shower running. Get dressed and wear your hair in that wet curly look," I told her. I knew there was a high chance of her messing her hair up so I didn't even want her to waste her time doing much to it.

"Come on baby, you know I don't like surprises." she whined. "How am I supposed to know what to put on, Chosen?"

"Dress for the beach." I gave her the biggest hint I could without spoiling the surprise. She was a water baby at heart. She was even a water sign. She loved nature but water was her absolute favorite. I knew anything I wanted to make special for her could be ten times more special if it was done by the water.

The moment I mentioned the beach, she jumped up and kissed me. I smiled to myself, knowing I had already made her happy before she even knew my plans. She was so appreciative that it made me want to do the unthinkable. I would tie a rope around the moon and drag it to earth for her. Anything to see her happy.

"Come on baby, we got to be there before seven," I told her as she ran off to get dressed.

It was like the moment she exited the room a dark cloud came over it. My phone started ringing back to back, instantly fucking up my mood.

Why the fuck is Choice calling me this early? I asked myself, beyond confused.

"Hello?" I answered the phone, trying not to express how tired I was of being hit up with everybody else's bullshit. Especially his bullshit.

"Man, some bullshit going on," Choice said.

"Tell me something I don't know," I responded dryly.

"Trice's ass done robbed me for like 200 grand. And the money not even mine, man. She trying to get me killed. And I'm convinced that Shawnie is the police." He immediately started shouting about a bunch of bullshit I didn't care to hear.

None of that shit had anything to do with me. I loved my brother, but I had to let him learn from his own mistakes. That was the only way to get his ass to stop doing dumb shit to end up in those type of situations.

"Look man, I think something bad finna happen," he told me.

"Like what?"

"I don't know, nigga. I'm telling you what I feel. And it's got something to do with Shawnie's ass. I just know it."

"Okay, what do you need from me?" I asked, not wanting to waste too much more of my time on his bullshit.

"I just need to hold some money so I can duck off till I can figure shit out," he said, still not realizing that money wasn't the answer to every problem.

"Look, I'm taking Vera out. I'll call you when I'm finished," I said before hanging up the phone. I wasn't even about to give that motherfucker no more time of my day.

"What's the matter?" Vera asked after walking in on me ending the call. I looked at her and smiled. It was crazy how her aura could just light up the entire room. I absolutely adored her. And there was literally nothing that could pull me away from her energy.

"Choice's ass calling me talking 'bout Trice robbed him and Shawnie his opp and shit," I explained our call in a nutshell. I was sure to put a little sarcasm in my tone to stop her from worrying about it.

"His ass is always up to something." She laughed.

"I'm finna turn my phone off on that nigga, man. I'on got time for nobody's drama today," I told her. She laughed again but we both knew I was as serious as a heart attack.

"I don't even blame you, honestly!" She started laughing again.

"You should turn yours off too. Let today just be our little getaway," I suggested to her before we headed to the car. She laughed it off but kept her phone on. See, Vera worried about other people's shit. I couldn't care less. She balanced my nonchalant approach to life. One of us had to care, but it damn sure wasn't about to be me.

CHAPTER THIRTY-SEVEN
VERA

My heart skipped a beat once Chosen and I arrived at the ocean. I absolutely loved the water and he knew that. I had no idea what he had planned but I was definitely happy about it. I took a moment to take in the scenery. The smell of the ocean, the sound of the waves, the sun baking my skin, the sand underneath my feet, the sight of seagulls flying around in harmony. Everything was just so beautiful.

"Thank you, baby!" I exclaimed before jumping into his arms. He wrapped his arms around me and smiled.

"You saying thank you and you don't even know what we doing yet," he replied in a joking manner, but I knew he was serious.

"Well, whatever we're doing, I'm down!" I told him as we made our way closer to the water.

"Are you sure about that?" he asked in a way that made me question what was coming next.

"What the hell is that supposed to mean?" I asked curiously.

The sound of a loud horn wailing in the distance snatched my attention for a brief second. I turned around and saw a huge yacht approaching us. I turned back to face him, wondering if it was coming for us.

"Is that... Did you?" I couldn't figure out how to ask the question, but he definitely understood it.

"Mmmmm hmmmm!" He nodded proudly. I couldn't help but to jump in his arms and wrap my legs around him. He always managed to make my days a little brighter. I couldn't be happier to have him all to myself.

"Are you still down?" he asked once he realized how emotional the yacht had made me. I turned around to face him and nearly fainted when I realized he was down on one knee. My man was proposing to me, on the beach while awaiting our yacht. I was so shocked that my tongue was tied up. I couldn't even think of what to say. I was literally speechless.

"Vera, you make every day brighter for me. In the middle of all the madness, you're always my peace. There isn't another woman I would even dream of being with over you. Please say you will be mine forever," he said, opening the ring box and exposing the big rock he got for my finger.

"Will you marry me?" He finally popped the question and I couldn't answer fast enough.

"Yes, yes, yes! Hell yes, I will!" I happily accepted him to have and to hold until death did us part. He jumped up to his feet and lifted me off mine. It was picture perfect, honestly. I don't think I've ever been happier in my entire life. I knew for sure I would never forget this day.

"You don't know how happy you just made me," he told me as we kissed passionately. Before we knew it, dozens of people had surrounded us and started taking pictures and cheering us on. It felt like the whole world was happy for us. And that feeling was well overdue for the both of us.

"Let's go celebrate," he said, grabbing my hand and jogging toward the yacht. I was amazingly surprised because I knew that he didn't trust being out in the open water. I knew this was something he was doing for me.

"Baby, we can stay here on the beach if you want," I suggested. I didn't want him stepping too far out of his comfort zone to where he couldn't enjoy it.

"Nah, it's cool baby. I've been practicing." He chuckled as we made our way to the boat.

Suddenly, out of nowhere my phone began to ring off the hook. It was my aunt Shaniece. I thought about answering it for a second, but the way Chosen mugged my phone made me reconsider.

"Whatever it is, it can wait," he said calmly. I agreed with him by smiling and placing my phone into my bag.

"You're right, baby," I told him as we both stepped into our new chapter of life together.

The deck on the boat was so beautiful. We sailed out to the middle of the ocean where we watched the sunset. I lusted over the way my man's skin glowed, even at night. He was so fine.

"You're mine forever!" he told me before wrapping me up in his arms. I melted in his embrace, taking in his scent and basking in his ambience.

"I love you so much," he told me as he continuously kissed my neck and ear. His touch was everything. His voice in my ear alone was enough to make me explode. Unable to control myself, I lifted my dress up and allowed my luscious ass to plop out. I felt his dick rock up immediately.

"Let's go to our room!" he whispered. I could tell he was shy about doing it in the open. But I wanted to push him. I wanted all his firsts to be with me.

"No, I want it now," I said, turning around and dropping to

my knees. I wasted no time pulling his thick, juicy rod out and shoving it down my throat.

"Fuckkkk!" he moaned in pleasure as I slurped him down. He caressed my hair and rubbed the side of my face as I let him fuck my face. I was so into him that my pussy was literally soaking through my thong.

"Come on," he demanded, pulling me up to my feet and bending me over the balcony.

"Oh, I love this dick!" I cried out as I felt him enter me. It was literally the sweetest pain I'd ever felt. I couldn't get enough of it. God, I loved me some him.

CHAPTER THIRTY-EIGHT
SHANIECE

I hadn't seen my husband in about five weeks. I knew right away that meant he was with another woman, and this was my last straw. We hadn't even fallen out or anything. It's like he just got overwhelmed with our life and ran off to go be with the next bitch. What was even crazier was that nobody had seen or heard from Trice and her kids for about the same amount of time as well.

I couldn't prove it, but I knew they were together. My intuition was so strong that I could sense their emotions for each other. They were falling hard for one another. Somehow, that scandalous little bitch had wiggled her way into bed with my husband.

A big part of me didn't want to believe it but my intuition was way too strong. I was certain I wasn't crazy. And the fact that they both had disappeared wasn't making matters any better.

I started to wonder where I went wrong and how things had ended up the way they were. I was a great wife to Dwayne. I was loyal, faithful, and I turned his ass into a boss. He hadn't ever touched real money until he met me. He just looked like it. But all in all, that man never had more than fifty grand in the bank before dealing with me. I made him into the man he was and now he was ready to drop me like a bad habit. I just couldn't understand it.

It felt like everyone was walking in their destiny and I was the only one being left behind, alone and in the dark. I thought of how much I would be giving up if I walked away from Dwayne and the crazy thing was, I couldn't come up with much. I was literally risking more holding on to him than I was letting go.

Wayne and his son had only brought confusion and trouble into the mix. I mean, yea, Wayne had set up the repast center, but after a while I realized that was something he did for himself. That's why he basically went away from me the moment that building was up and running. I didn't trust him one bit. I was certain he had been using me now and thought I was going to sit back comfortably and watch him spoil the next woman after I had put him in the position to do so. He definitely had me fucked up.

Desperate to get out of my thoughts, I decided to check my emails. There wasn't anything major in there but I did see an email from Detective Randolph. It was an old email stating he needed to ask us questions a few months back. The email itself naturally made me think about the young man Latrell who was illegally disposed of thanks to my services. I couldn't get his picture out of my head and I thought about him way more than a little bit.

Not even sure what I was looking for, I decided to Google his name. I wanted to know more about his story. I felt such a connection to him from the moment I saw him laying lifeless on that table that I couldn't forget about him. And I was positive he wasn't the only one. But for some reason he was hard to forget.

After a couple more minutes of scrolling through the internet, I came up on something that made me damn near faint right then and there.

"This is her fucking son?" I said after seeing the article about a mother in search of her missing son. The picture was clear as day, Shawnie and Latrell. It didn't take me too much longer to learn that she was a cop from a different jurisdiction either.

"Oh my fucking god!" I gasped once I realized how deep Choice had us into shit. I wondered if I should warn them or just make a run on my own. Technically, I didn't have anything to do with the shit and I could prove it.

On top of that, my husband was having an affair with our daughter-in-law. I don't care how a motherfucker looked at it. Nobody could convince me differently. Honestly, I was thinking of letting them all burn. But the bigger part of me wouldn't let me.

"Let me go see Vera," I thought out loud as I headed to my door. I knew at least if I told her, she could tell Chosen and whatever happened from there was out of my hand. At least I would have done my part. I left out my house in a hurry, only to be stopped in my tracks.

"What the fuck are you doing at my house?" I asked, offended, after seeing Shawnie and Raj standing on my front porch.

"We need to speak. We can either do it here or you can come downtown," she said, flashing me her badge.

"Oh, you not undercover no more?" I asked sarcastically, letting her know I already knew she was a cop and didn't give a fuck.

"Choice is yours!" Raj added. I looked at him and then back to Shawnie.

"They got to have a reason for coming here," I told myself as I stepped back and gestured for them to come inside.

"That's my girl," Shawnie said sarcastically. "I knew I liked you for a reason," she added as they stepped into my house.

CHAPTER THIRTY-NINE
SHAWNIE

"You're probably wondering what I'm doing here, huh?" I asked Shaniece as I took a seat on her sofa. She looked at me like she was dumb and I shook my head irritably.

"Can we get to it?" she asked with the audacity to sound as if I was getting on her nerves. In all honesty, she was a little nervous. I could see it and I was positive she didn't want us to know that.

"Sure thing," I said with a smile while extending my hand out to Raj. He smiled and nodded at her before handing her a manila envelope. I knew she thought she knew exactly who Raj was. I knew so much about Shaniece that I staged everything she found out about Raj during her little identity check. So everything she thought she knew about him was his under-cover profile.

"You seem like the scratch my back and I'll scratch yours kind of person," I said before pulling pictures out of the envelope.

"But you also seem like one of those don't fuck me over

type women," I added before handing Shaniece the pictures. I could tell a small part of her was afraid to look at those pictures, and rightfully so.

"What the hell is this?" she asked, taking the pictures out of my hand but not flipping them over. I just smiled at her. I had been watching their family so tough that I knew about Trice and Wayne's affair before it even started. I had hired private investigators to watch that entire circle, all in hope of finding my son. I had dirt on every single person tied to Wettler's and I was about to shake their foundation up with it.

Shaniece looked at the pictures and almost fainted when she saw Dwayne and Trice hugging and kissing. It was passionate kissing too. Like they loved each other. I could tell, and Shaniece could to. It broke my heart to see Shaniece's heart break right in front of me because I knew that pain. But if that's what I had to do to get answers, then that's what I was going to do.

"What's your point in showing me this?" Shaniece asked nonchalantly, thinking that we couldn't see her sweat. It was taking everything in her to hold herself together. Deep down, she was falling apart and that's exactly what I needed her to be doing. I watched as her mood went from heart broken to enraged. It looked like she wanted to run out of that house and go murder Dwayne and Trice that very second.

"My point is, I see that you're loyal and faithful but it's to the wrong motherfuckers. Your little crew is about to sink and I'on want you to go down with them. You don't deserve this. On top of that, all that shit is in your name. You're going to go down while them motherfuckers get out and be happy together," I added, pointing to the pictures and using her husband's affair as ammo. And I'm not gone lie, it was definitely some good ammo. Shit had her hot as hell.

"Look, I just want justice for my son. Raj here wants his

200K that Choice stole back, and I'm sure you want to keep your business up and running."

"What exactly do you need from me?" Shaniece asked.

"You give me Choice, I'll get rid of Dwayne."

"What do you mean get rid of him?" she asked skeptically.

"I'll make sure he does the time and not you. And I'll promise protection for Wettler's."

"We keep the whole side business thing in the dark?" she asked curiously. I could tell she was fearful of something like that getting out.

"Absolutely. All you need to do is get me Choice," I assured her.

"You blew your cover?" she asked, confused. I could tell that she was wondering why I needed anybody else to get to Choice now when I had literally just had him wrapped around my finger.

"Yes, my cover has been blown. The part you should be concerned about is the fact that Choice hasn't reported it to you or y'all's family. He has some shit up his sleeve. He's planning on pinning all of this on you and your husband. It's his way of getting revenge for you killing his mom and his dad stealing his wife." I quickly fabricated a story using bits and pieces of truth I had already heard. I knew the little bit of truth in the story was going to win her over.

"I'll do it!" Shaniece said with tears in her eyes. It was so easy to persuade her that her family was against her because they all were always doing some skeptical shit to each other.

"Great, I have the perfect plan," I said matter-of-factly as I scooted an inch closer to her. My plan was vacuum sealed. There was literally no way to fuck it up. For starters, I was going to use every little secret I knew about them to turn everyone against each other. And since everyone was hiding something, nobody would even think to mention any side business they had going with me because they were already doing something they ain't have no business doing.

I was going to use Shaniece to get Choice's ass gone because I knew she didn't like his ass no way. With her help, I was going to send Dwayne off to prison to please the judge, and when I was finished, I was going to kill Shaniece as well. Vera, Chosen, everybody. I was even coming after their company. Shaniece was an absolute fool for trusting me. Everybody in that family was going to wish they hadn't crossed paths with my son. I was going to be sure of that if it was the last thing I ever did!

CHAPTER FORTY
WAYNE

"You dog ass nigga. You really thought I wasn't going to find out about you fucking Trice?" my wife screamed at me through the phone. I immediately woke all the way up.

"Shaniece, what the fuck are you talking about?" I asked, confused as to why she thought I was fucking Trice. In all actuality, I hadn't even fucked her yet. But I knew it was going to happen. I just didn't understand how she knew it was going to happen. I hadn't told anybody anything about Trice so it was a surprise to me that Shaniece was even saying that to me.

"You dirty, scandalous bitch!" she screamed at the top of her lungs. It was obvious that she was beyond hurt. She had never spoken to me that way. Honestly, I didn't know what to say.

"I made you, motherfucker. I made you a motherfuckin' millionaire and you want to run off with your son's wife? What about your son? I can't believe you!"

"Listen, you don't know what the fuck you're talking

about. Somebody lied to you," I tried to explain my side to her but she was too upset.

"And you had the nerve to give that bitch five thousand dollars of my money! You and that bitch can die. I'm going to make sure your broke ass don't get another penny out of me. All our joint accounts are closed. So hopefully that bitch got some money for you!" she hissed.

Normally a threat like that would send me ticking, but not this time around. I honestly didn't give a damn about her money because I already had my shit going on the side. I was already secure enough to stay afloat if she ever jumped ship on me. You would think that she would know that.

"You're doing all this over a lie, man." I tried one last time to tell her the truth. I knew how powerful my wife was and I really wasn't trying to be on her bad side over a rumor.

"Oh, it's a lie? Watch this!" she said before getting quiet. I waited to see what was next, and then the pictures started coming through my phone.

"What the fuck?" I accidentally let my thoughts slip my mind as I skipped through multiple pictures of me and Trice going at it. It most definitely looked like we fucked, but I was just proving a point to her. But I knew there was no way to get Shaniece to see that. She was going to believe what she saw on the pictures and not what actually happened. And no matter what, she was still going to be mad.

"Look, it's not what it looks like," I started to try and explain, but she cut me off.

"Fuck you, Dwayne. I'ma make sure you, your son, and that bitch all burn together," she yelled in a fit before hanging up the phone.

"Is everything okay?" Trice asked after hearing bits and pieces of my conversation. I looked at her and shook my head no.

"I don't know how it happened, but Shaniece has pictures of us kissing and she is convinced we're having an affair," I explained to Trice.

"What? How? We only kissed that one time." She was just as confused as me.

"I don't know and I don't care. I really fuck with you. You been my peace lately and more of a wife than Shaniece. You don't know how much I enjoy being with you. I'll really fall out with everybody about it. I just be wanting to be around you for real!" I confessed.

"You mean that?" she asked cautiously as if she didn't trust me.

"Yes," I said seriously before placing a kiss on her lips.

"I don't want to cause problems between you and your wife. I'm not a home wrecker."

"That's not a home. I feel more at home with you. I'll fall out with whoever behind it. I just need to know that you feel the same way about me. I need to know if you gone thug this out with me."

"Honestly, I don't want to leave you. Our connection is so real. I can't be without you now. I've been feeling that way and just wasn't able to tell you."

"I don't want you to leave," I added. "I want you to let me into your heart, Trice. I want your trust. I want you to be mine. Completely. And I want to give you the same in return. You think you ready for that type of commitment?" I played the wild card.

"You mean that?" she asked with tears pooling in her eyes.

"Every word!"

"You don't care about what Choice and Shaniece gone say?"

"It don't matter. We don't have to see them. If they don't like it, they don't like it. But I'm not gone ignore the way I feel about you. This shit is only getting stronger!" I added before kissing her again. I pulled her up by her arm so that she was facing me. Eye to eye. "You sure this is what you want?" I asked as I moved in closer to her. "You don't got to play games with me, Trice."

"I'm serious. I won't play with you," she replied genuinely.

I paused. This time I could see that Trice was a little intimidated by my loss of words. She needed me to say something. I answered her curiosity by cupping her chin and leaning in to kiss her. It was passionate. Hard. Perfect. The only thing that felt right in the middle of so much chaos. I stared at her, watching her reaction as I slowly began to remove her clothing. I needed to get inside of her head. I needed her to feel loved. I needed her trust.

"You sure you serious about this?" I kissed her neck and then her collar bone. "After this, it ain't no turning back. You sure this what you want?" I stopped to face her once again before slipping out of my pants and boxers. She nodded hungrily.

"Yes, Wayne." I stared at her one more time just before I entered her. Her love box was so tight and wet that I almost forgot she wasn't my wife. I wanted to blast off in her right away. In my mind we were already married with two kids.

I was seriously falling for her. Her expression alone drove me wild and I could tell she was honestly enjoying every second of me being inside her. She moaned at the very rough but gentle way I handled her. My strokes were slow, long, and passionate. I took my time, careful not to hurt her with my size.

I grabbed her by her hips, pulling her closer to me. For a brief moment, she tried to scoot away from the deliciously sharp pains. It was becoming too much for her, but I held her in place. The pain quickly became pleasure. Over and over again as we became one. She grabbed my back and held on to me. I could feel soft groans forming in my throat. A sense of satisfaction and pride came over her when she heard me moaning. Suddenly, it became more than sex for both of us.

"Tell me it's mine," I demanded. She wasted no time answering me.

"It's yours, Wayne. It's yours!" she found herself repeatedly screaming over and over.

"I'm serious!" I whispered in between strokes. I grabbed her face to redirect her gaze to mine. "Say it again." My tone was deep but still weak from that good ass pussy she was putting on me.

"It's yours, Wayne." She continued to scream until we both reached our orgasms. And as hard as I tried to, I simply couldn't pull out of her. We laid together, panting and still trying to comprehend the fact that we had really done what we did together. It was wrong, but I didn't care. The way Trice made me feel was worth all the drama that was coming.

CHAPTER FORTY-ONE
CHOICE

I stood in my bedroom trying not to panic. I had always been ready for whatever, but no one could have prepared me for the day that motherfuckers would be coming to my home. I tried to think of what moves to make first, but I knew I was running out of time.

"Shit!" I barked out. I was slowly starting to lose my cool. Panic was starting to become my only option. And to be honest, I was a little scared. I knew if motherfuckers were serious enough to come to my house then that meant they meant business. I hurriedly grabbed my phone and called my brother. I needed at least one person to know who to go after if shit went super left.

"Wassup Choice?" Chosen answered the phone in such good spirits. I instantly began to wish I was in his shoes instead of my own. But it was life and if I got out of this situation alive, I was most definitely about to switch up a whole lot of shit.

"Bro, if anything happens, it's Shawnie and that nigga Raj," I told him.

"What? What you mean?" The happiness immediately left his tone and was replaced with concern.

"Where are you at, Choice?"

"I'm at the crib. Shawnie and Raj just pulled up to my crib with they guns out."

"They didn't come in?"

"Nah, I think they are scoping the place out or something."

"What are they doing together?" Chosen was just as confused as me. The sad thing was I couldn't even answer him. I had never seen them together outside of our meetings but from the way they pulled up, they definitely were closer than I thought.

There was all types of shit that turned out to be something other than what I thought. Especially when it came to Shawnie's ass. I fell hard for that girl and the whole time she was just playing games with me. I left my family for her and all and she never even had plans on being with me. She had hella secrets and bad intentions from the jump. Shawnie really played the fuck out of me and I deserved it for how I did Trice. One thing was for sure, Trice damn sure wouldn't be pulling up to my house with another nigga to bring me any harm.

In that moment, I started to miss the fuck out of Trice. It saddened my heart to consider I may not ever see her again. I may not ever get the chance to right my wrongs with her and show her how much I regretted leaving her. If I could turn back the hands of time, I would be back home with my family. I shouldn't have ever taken them for granted. Especially not for no scandalous ass bitch like Shawnie.

"Yea, somebody def just came in this motherfucker," I whispered to my brother after I heard the sound of someone breaking into my house.

"Whatever happens, I love you!" I said honestly. I was always in the mix of shit, so much so to the point where I hadn't really told my family that I loved them. Everything was just about money. Now I was starting to regret all that.

"I love you too. I'm on the way!" Chosen told me. I could tell he was tearing up and could hear a lump forming in his throat. He was scared for me too.

In an attempt to record whatever went down, I left my phone sitting on the dresser without hanging it up. At least that way Chosen would be able to hear what the fuck was going on.

"So you the nigga Choice?" I heard an unfamiliar male voice speaking. I turned to see an unfamiliar black man standing in my room door.

"Aye, who the fuck is you?" I said with my gun aimed at him already.

"He don't even know who I am?" He chuckled to Shawnie as she came from behind him and joined his side.

"Shawnie, what the fuck?" I was so lost. Like this bitch had a whole nigga but was staying with me and everything.

"This is my baby's father, Scar," Shawnie proudly introduced us.

"Man, what the fuck is going on?" I asked even more confused than I was at first.

"Scar and I are here for vengeance. And Raj is here too. He's looking for the money you stole," Shawnie said matter-of-factly.

"Vengeance for what? I ain't never even did shit to you, Shawnie."

"Not to her," Scar pitched in. "To our son!" he added before pointing his gun at me. I froze for a second. I realized it was either me or them. Or all of us. Either way, I wasn't going out without a fight.

TO BE CONTINUED...

DEAR VALUED READERS

First and foremost, I want to express my deepest gratitude to each and every one of you for supporting Cole Hart Signature books. Your enthusiasm, loyalty, and passion for the stories we create is the fuel that drives our success. We are immensely grateful for your continued dedication and encouragement, which has made it possible for us to bring our worlds to life in the pages of our books.

As we continue to grow and evolve, your feedback is invaluable to us. We are eager to hear your thoughts and opinions on our work, and we hope you will take a moment to leave us an honest review on Amazon and/or Goodreads. Your insights not only help us improve and refine our craft but also allow fellow readers to discover and enjoy the magic of our stories.

We also kindly ask you to share your favorite Cole Hart Signature books with friends, family, and on your social media pages. Word of mouth is an incredibly powerful way to support us and help our community of readers grow. By sharing your love for our books, you are not only championing our work but also contributing to a vibrant, diverse, and passionate literary community.

Once again, thank you for your unwavering support and for being a part of our journey. We couldn't do this without you, and we promise to keep delivering exciting, immersive, and unforgettable stories for you to enjoy.

With heartfelt appreciation,

Author and Creator
Cole Hart Signature Books

ALSO BY EVONNA

The Essence Of A Side Chick

Made in the USA
Middletown, DE
05 July 2023

34598488R00102